As the funeral service began, Frost looked around surveying his company. There were thirty troops in the motorcycle patrol, and the third trooper closest to the President caught his eye. There was something about the soldier that was wrong. Suddenly he saw the muzzle of the trooper's M-16 waver, then sweep downward toward President Aguillara-Garcia.

Frost tried to remember the Spanish words for "Look out," but they wouldn't come. There was time for only one thing, so he threw himself forward, his left hand slapping the muzzle of the trooper's gun upward, his right knee smashing the soldier's groin.

Frost's right knee connected and the assassin started to fall back. Taking a half step forward, Frost released the rifle and crashed his left elbow into the soldier's jaw. Then he drove his right fist in a straight karate blow aimed at his adversary's Adam's apple, crushing his windpipe. Frost ripped the M-16 free as the trooper fell back, already dead, into the open grave of the brother of the President whom he had just tried to murder.

And as the President rushed over to thank him, Frost knew that this incident was the first of many to come . . .

SPECTACULAR SERIES

NAZI INTERROGATOR   (649, $2.95)
by Raymond F. Toliver
The terror, the fear, the brutal treatment, and mental torture of
WWII prisoners are all revealed in this first-hand account of the
Luftwaffe's master interrogator.

THE SGT. #3: BLOODY BUSH   (647, $2.25)
by Gordon Davis
In this third exciting episode, Sgt. C.J. Mahoney is put to his
deadliest test when he's assigned to bail out the First Battalion in
Normandy's savage Battle of the Hedgerows.

SHELTER #3: CHAIN GANG KILL   (658, $1.95)
by Paul Ledd
Shelter finds himself "wanted" by a member of the death battalion who double-crossed him seven years before *and* by a fiery
wench. Bound by lust, Shelter aims to please; burning with
vengeance, he seeks to kill!

GUNN #3: DEATH'S HEAD TRAIL   (648, $1.95)
by Jory Sherman
When Gunn stops off in Bannack City he finds plenty of gold,
girls, and a gunslingin' outlaw who wants it all. With his hands on
his holster and his eyes on the sumptuous Angela Larkin, Gunn
goes off hot—on his enemy's trail!

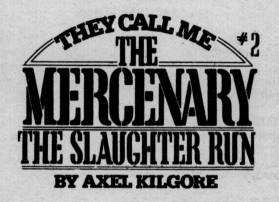

THEY CALL ME #2
THE
MERCENARY
THE SLAUGHTER RUN
BY AXEL KILGORE

ZEBRA BOOKS
KENSINGTON PUBLISHING CORP.

ZEBRA BOOKS

are published by

KENSINGTON PUBLISHING CORP.
21 East 40th Street
New York, N.Y. 10016

Printed in the United States of America

For Joe Rosenberger—
The Professor's Been Paid, My Friend

Any resemblance to persons living or dead is purely coincidental.

Chapter One

The wind was starting to blow up hard as Hank Frost stood on the brow of the isolated slope, watching the reddish orange orb of sun start to sink low toward the tree line, the pines offering what modest protection there was from the ice spicules pounding like tiny needles against the exposed skin of his cheeks and forehead. "At least my eyepatch will keep me warm," he said, but to no one in particular. Frost was alone—very alone—he thought, snapping away the butt of the burnt-to-the-fingertips Camel he'd been smoking while thinking about Bess. A plane was flying overhead, a commercial jet, but it was only in books and movies, he reflected, that as the hero stood on the icy mountaintop the heroine would be sitting wistfully aboard the aircraft flying overhead—lovers, star-crossed and so close but yet so far! He closed his thoughts by verbalizing the word, "Bullshit" and pulled his ski mask from the pocket of his jacket. Bess, he thought, though he loved her dearly, wasn't exactly what you'd call the "wistful" type.

She was on her way back to London, picking up where she'd left off with her bureau for the news service. And Frost was on his way to nowhere in particular at the moment—right where he'd left off. He wasn't really being quite fair to himself, he thought. He was actually on his way to somewhere—the next day he'd be rejoining Diablo Protective Services, the executive protection group he usually worked for between mercenary jobs— "Diablo Fights Like The Devil—For You." At least that was their slogan, he recalled. Everyone couldn't be Shakespeare. But they were a good outfit and always eager to include Frost on their far-flung assignments. A little rest guarding some overrich businessman from bogeymen would do him good, Frost reasoned.

Frost's back had required the minor surgery originally suspected, but he was long over it now and having no difficulties. But as Bess had warned him, her mother instinct irrepressible, he was still supposed to take things a little easy. Unfortunately, however, that didn't quite go along with his bank balance. He was down to less than ten thousand dollars, his Browning High Power, two Gerber knives, an Omega wristwatch, and assorted clothes he sincerely felt he would have had to pay a charity drive to haul away. And Diablo Protective Services paid on time, and well.

As Frost bent to adjust the bindings on his skis— what the doctor who'd worked on his back didn't know wouldn't hurt him—he thought he heard someone talking. He turned and looked to his left. There, by the stand of trees separating him from the main ski run, he thought. As he bent to the other binding, he heard the talking again. Staying there, crouched, he remained perfectly motionless.

He watched the slender second hand sweep one revolution on the black face of his Omega Seamaster 120, hearing no other sound than the faint ticking of the watch and the wind. And it was the wind playing tricks on him, Frost thought. But as he started to get up, he heard a cry and just before that, he would have sworn he'd heard a popping sound, like a cork from a small bottle of champagne. Then he heard the popping sound again.

It could have been a bottle of champagne shared by two clandestine lovers he thought, or a branch bending under the weight of the snowfall from the previous evening perhaps. It could have been any of those things or a million things like them, he thought. Or it could have been the sound of a primer detonation on a silenced pistol.

Feeling under his ski jacket with his exposed left hand that the Gerber MkI boot knife was where it should be, Frost secured the last binding on his skis and edged to the left across the snow toward the tree line.

He side-stepped to get some elevation on where he'd pinpointed the sound—not wanting to suddenly find himself right in the middle of something if indeed what he had heard had been gunshots. Using his ski poles for added support, digging in with the uphill sides of his skis, it took him perhaps three minutes to cross the forty or fifty yards to the tree line. Staring down toward where he had heard the sound, at first Frost could see nothing. But then, he caught a flash of movement—something dark outlined against the white snow background. He saw it again a second later—the shape was a pistol.

As he leaned forward, his right ski—the down-hill one—slipped and he caught himself against the slender trunk of a pine tree, the force of his aborted fall shaking the conifer and dislodging some of the freshly fallen snow from its heavily laden branches.

As Frost got himself up on balance, he glanced back, down to where he'd seen the pistol. There was a man standing beside the trees now, ski-clad feet apart, a slender-barreled automatic with a sausage-shaped silencer—awkward-looking there at its muzzle—in his right hand.

Frost stared at the man for a split second, then dug his poles into the snow and launched himself down the slope straight toward the gunman. The man raised the pistol to fire, but, too late. Frost plowed into him and knocked him sprawling into the snow. As Frost skied past, he shot a glance toward the trees—there was a second man with a gun, and beside that man Frost saw a body, unmoving and facedown in the snow. Frost dug in his poles, did a christie and shot off to his right into the tree line, slowed abruptly as he reached it, heard a bullet ricocheting off one of the trees near him and dug in his poles again.

Back on the ski slope where he'd started now, Frost christied and stopped. He could see the first of the two gunmen firing at him, though he could hear no shots—they were professional guns, he reflected bitterly. Both men had skis and the gunman who wasn't firing was already starting to dig in his poles and give chase.

Frost shot a glance down the slope—it was steep and fast and the sort of slope he usually avoided, at least at any speed. Frost stabbed his poles into the snow and shoved himself off, pulling his body down into a head-forward tuck to cut his wind resistance and bracing the ski poles under his arms to get them out of the way. Shooting a glance over his right shoulder, he could see the first of the two gunmen not a hundred yards behind him, the second man, presumably still firing at him, still back by the tree line.

Catapulting down the mountainside along the unfamiliar ski trail, Frost's mind raced. Two men just killed a third, both men armed with silenced pistols, likely .22s, both guys probably professionals. Good, he thought. Professional killers weren't usually noted for physical fitness, at least not the crime syndicate type. If these men were KGB or something similar, on the other hand, they could also be qualified mountain troopers—and that was bad. Frost glanced behind him again—the gunman was gaining, but just a little.

As Frost looked ahead of him, he could see the trail starting to narrow, the tree line on both sides closing in, then a sign, "No Skiing Beyond Next Marker." Wonderful, he thought. At the speed he was traveling, the next marker was less than a minute away from him—he could see it. Glancing behind him again, he could see the gunman moving up fast.

Frost christied left and shot toward the nearest tree line, thinking if he couldn't outrun the gunman he'd outmaneuver him. As Frost reached the trees, he skied down along beside them for twenty-five yards then cut through again, just as the gunman was cutting across the tree line for the first time. Frost stopped himself abruptly in the trees and waited, perfectly still. The second gunman still wasn't in sight, but Frost presumed he was on the way—either that or he had taken the ski lift down the mountain to intercept Frost if he eluded the first gunman and got that far.

Waiting quietly, Frost broke open the thumb snap on the Gerber boot knife's sheath and quickly cut away the thongs on both of his ski poles. Inverting one of the poles, he used the thongs and

14

lashed the green catspaw-surfaced handle of the knife below the basket, running alongside the point of the pole.

Frost had carefully skied down some twenty yards past his current position, then as neatly as possible backtracked twenty yards above his position, this to confuse his tracks and keep the gunman from pinpointing his position.

Frost could hear nothing, except the keening sound of the wind. He had no idea from which side the gunman would come, nor any idea exactly where the gunman was at that instant. The ski pole with the Gerber knife lashed to it held at high port in front of him—a field expedient spear—he waited.

Frost heard a faint crunching sound in the snow to his left, wheeled and the ski-masked, black-clad gunman was six feet from him, the pistol on line with Frost's chest. There was no time for anything fancy, Frost thought. He dove forward, shifting the ski pole spear quickly to his left hand and driving forward toward his enemy's chest. The gunman started to sidestep and Frost felt a searing pain across the top of his left shoulder, but continued his lunge, the point of the Gerber knife plunging into the gunman's upper chest cavity, missing the throat—his target.

As the gunman started to reel back, Frost stepped toward him, wrenching the improvised spear from the gunman's chest and then hammering it downward. The gunman was feebly drawing his hand across his face and neck, but

Frost continued the thrust, the point of the knife biting through the gunman's left wrist, coming out the other side and entering the man's throat at the Adam's apple, pinioning the wrist to the neck. With his mouth opened wide, the dead man looked as though he had died of shock.

As Frost withdrew the knife and wiped it clean of blood against the man's clothes, he reflected that maybe the gunman had died of shock. Frost caught up the dead man's pistol and brushed it clean of snow. A Colt Woodsman, the post-war model with adjustable rear sight and the 4¾-inch barrel, the silencer a Sionics. There was a custom slide lock on the Woodsman for single-shot use with the silencer at maximum efficiency. Frost thumbed the base of the butt release and withdrew the magazine—four rounds remained, .22 Long Rifle solids. As Frost rubbed his shoulder—a flesh wound he suspected, the bullet just creasing the skin and not imbedding—he was grateful he hadn't found that the bullets were poisoned. He looked over the gun carefully. The place where the serial number should have been was pock-marked with shallow drillholes, the number permanently obliterated—one form of "sanitizing."

Frost searched the dead man's pockets, kneeling beside him there in the white snow already staining red with the killer's blood from the two knife wounds. All Frost found was one spare magazine for the Woodsman and a Swiss Army Knife. There was no identification. He ripped away the ski mask. The face, locked forever in a rictus of pain, was Slavic-looking, but he couldn't be sure of origin. Instinctively, though, he pegged the man as European, perhaps Latin American, but not North American or Canadian. The features just weren't right. Frost pulled off the man's gloves. Scars on the fingertips seemed to indicate the dead man had once either been a very clumsy butcher or tried tampering with his fingerprints.

Frost stood up, dumped the magazine already half emptied into his ski jacket pocket, checked the chambered round and put the fresh ten-round magazine in place. He made sure the sidelock was off so the pistol would fire in the semiautomatic mode, then gave the silencer or suppressor—the names were essentially synonymous—a good luck twist. He shoved the gun inside his trouser band. Freeing his knife from the ski pole and pocketing the thongs he'd used, he sheathed the knife, took a last look around him for the second gunman—nothing—and then took off again down the slope. As he picked up speed and started crisscrossing the slope to keep the speed under control, Frost knew full well the second man would be waiting for him by the lift station below.

It took better than twenty minutes at the rate he was going to reach the lift area. The wrong time of the year, there were few skiers in view. He christied again, dug in his poles and ground to a stop in a spray of powdery snow. Herringboning up a small slope, he stopped and loosened the bindings on his skis and picked them up, shouldering them. There

17

were at least a half dozen men in dark clothes wearing ski masks—the weather was cold and because it was now nearly dark, the wind was picking up in intensity. Frost started walking toward the small, antiseptic-looking restaurant at the base of the lift station.

He left his skis in the outside rack, not really worrying if they would be stolen since they were rented anyway, and stepped inside. He pulled off the toque mask he wore and pocketed it, but left his jacket zipped to hide the butt of the silenced Woodsman carried crossdraw in his trouser waistband.

He walked past the small tables in the interior portion of the restaurant and out onto the windswept veranda. There were a very few other hardy souls out there as well, couples mostly, looking for privacy. As a shivering waiter went by, Frost flagged him down and ordered coffee, then selected one of the myriad empty tables and sat down. Lighting a cigarette, he looked off across the slope, dotted here and there with indefinable dark shapes of skiers who were either good enough to keep to the snow when it was getting dark or too foolish to know that they shouldn't.

Frost paid the waiter when he brought the coffee, then picked up the steaming mug and walked toward the balcony overlooking the lift area. He could see several likely candidates for the second gunman, but with the cold there was nothing sinister about someone keeping his ski mask in place against it.

But one of the men, as Frost studied the scene,

almost inhaling the coffee he clutched in both bared hands for the warmth it afforded, was pointing up toward him, pointing Frost out to a woman in a robin's egg blue ski parka, her hood up against the winds, concealing her face and hair. Frost saw the woman nodding to the man in the ski mask then looking up toward him again.

Frost did the only thing that seemed sensible. He waved to the woman and after an over-long pause, the woman waved back, held up one finger gesturing for him to wait, then started off at a trot for the lower level entrance to the restaurant.

Frost hailed his waiter, ordered a fresh coffee for himself and then a coffee for the lady—already he could see her making her way across the restaurant toward him, the hood from the parka down and the coat partially unzipped. Her face was young, pretty and alert, her eyes almost a pansy color of blue.

She walked straight toward Frost and stopped in front of him. "I'm sorry I don't know your name," she said.

"I'm sorry too," Frost responded. "I ordered coffee for us both, terribly cold now isn't it?"

"Yes," she said, matter-of-factly.

When the waiter arrived, Frost handed her one of the mugs and she took it.

"You know why I'm here?" she asked.

"Uh-huh, yeah—I know. You know what happened to your other pal, back there on the snow?"

"Yes, either you're a talented amateur or very professional."

19

"Why don't we say I'm a talented professional amateur. You looking for the same, kid?" Frost lit a cigarette, offering one to the woman.

She nodded negative, saying, "Bad for your health, Mr.—?"

"I know, Miss—?"

"Hmmm, now how should I go about getting you someplace where I can kill you?"

"The hell if I know—I suppose we could always wait until the place cleans out, then you could kill me, vault over the rail here and make your escape."

"I'm not much at vaulting."

"Aww, just goes to show how wrong you can be about someone," Frost said. "When I looked at you the first time, I said now there's a vaulter if I ever saw one. Looks like I'm fresh out of ways for you to kill me—sorry."

Frost smiled and made a mock toast with his coffee cup.

"You are a professional, aren't you, but you're alone?"

"What's that French philosopher talk about—aren't we all alone in the universe?" Frost smiled.

"Come on, you want a lot of innocent people to get hurt?"

"Doesn't bother me—I don't know any of them," Frost lied, playing his tough guy routine to the hilt. "But I'll tell you one thing, make a play here and you're going to be sorry there aren't more of you."

The girl had kept her right glove on all through their dialogue, but Frost had noticed her pulling it off while she was still outside before she entered the restaurant. If she made the move to shake his hand or touch his cheek, he knew what to expect.

And almost immediately she started going into her move. She tugged at her right glove and just as he'd expected, there was a large, very beautiful ring on her finger.

Standing beside him against the balcony railing, she started reaching for his hand. And just as she was about to make contact, he grabbed her right hand in his and twisted it over. She almost screamed, he could hear her stifling the sound.

The ring had a spring-loaded needle point in the base of the band, apparently activated by one of the stones that was in reality a switch analogous to a push-button knife.

"Let go of my hand," she gasped.

"Why, so you can stick me with that thing and walk away while I sink to the floor and die—no thank you."

"Let go, damn you—you're hurting me."

"Oh, please don't say that. To think that I'd hurt you just for a little thing like you trying to kill me—tsk, tsk," Frost said, smiling.

"What do you want?"

"What have you got?"

"Damn you—give me a straight answer."

"Okay—ask me a straight question."

"What are you going to do?" she asked, trying to free her wrist, Frost gripping it all the more tightly.

"What am I going to do with you? Fair question," he answered, thoughtfully. "Kill you." Smiling, he started to raise her hand from the rail

21

and bring it toward her throat or face. She started to scream and he hooked his arm around her and pulled her close to him and kissed her. She tried biting his lips, then let him kiss her, then started kissing him back. All the while, Frost held the right wrist and as their lips parted he squeezed her right palm against her left. Smiling at her as her eyes grew wide in fear of the inevitable, imminent death, he said, "I'm really not as callous as I've led you to believe. Truly," he whispered, as he guided her toward a chair—she could barely walk. "I am sorry."

He propped her in the chair, her left arm against the railing and her head resting near her elbow. She closed her eyes and died.

Frost glanced over his shoulder, bent to feign whispering in her ear, then made a show of telling her good-bye and walked away, pulling on his ski mask as he walked back through the restaurant and out into the snow. His rented skis were where he'd left them. Mentally, he balanced the virtues of the other man having taken them—there were none. Frost could easily have stolen a pair to replace them, and likely the gunman waiting for him somewhere outside was expecting the blonde-haired girl in the blue parka, now dead, to have finished him off.

Frost hoisted his skis onto his left shoulder and in long strides made his way through the sparse crowd of skiers toward the lift. Although he assumed there was only one gunman, Frost had no way of being sure. His plan was to take the ski lift back down the mountainside for the town, then get to his hired car and make it back to Zurich as soon as possible. If anything else came of the assassination he had witnessed earlier on the mountainside, any legal or extra-legal complications, at least in Zurich he had CIA contacts and was on what could pass for home turf, having now spent four months there living with Bess.

Frost had the stub from the two-way lift ticket he'd bought earlier that day on the way up, showed it to the ticket seller and walked through the turnstyle, then walked toward the platform. There was no lift, but as he scanned the mountainside in both directions—up and down—he could see one of the gondolas approaching, coming toward him down the mountain.

Frost glanced behind him. This time, there was no mistaking the black-clad man with the ski mask, pointing excitedly in his direction to two other men. Still, nothing was coming from below. As the gondola pulled into the lift station and passengers began boarding to head up the summit, most without skis since darkness was approaching and it seemed more a party crowd, Frost made his decision.

Breaking into a run, he reached the upward-bound gondola and secured his skis, then entered the lift. No more than a dozen people were inside as the operator pushed the doors closed and fingered the button to start the lift back toward the summit.

Behind them, as the lift bellied down, started groaning into the ascent, Frost could see the ski-masked gunman and the two men with him, wearing ski masks as well. They were waiting on the lift platform on the opposite side for the next gondola. Glancing ahead through the partially frosted over gondola window, Frost could see the next gondola approaching and about to pass his own. With luck, at the outside, the gunmen would be five minutes behind him.

Frost wove his way past the other lift passengers and looked back down the slope. As the second gondola reached the station, a swarm of down-mountain passengers disembarking, Frost spotted one of the gunmen walk toward the lift operator standing on the platform, move very close to him and then shove the man toward the lift. The other two gunmen, Frost made out, were stepping inside, pushing the remaining lift passengers back onto the platform. And then the gondola started up the mountain.

Frost glanced forward in his own gondola. There seemed to be no varying speed for the lift on the control panel the operator was standing beside. The lift had twelve passengers, plus Frost himself and the lift operator. The gondola coming up fast behind them now on the parallel cable was burdened with only three passengers and an operator—as Frost started calculating the difference in speed, he glanced back. The gondola was moving rapidly and, Frost estimated, should overtake the one he rode just prior to reaching the top of the slope.

The passengers around him were a mixed lot—young and old, male and female.

The strategy of his pursuers was easy to grasp.

Come up parallel to the gondola in which he rode, open fire and gun him down, then take the lift back down the mountainside, kill the operator, and make their escape. Trouble was, Frost realized, perhaps all the innocent people aboard his lift would be killed when the bullets flew.

Almost bitterly, he remembered his comment to the woman back at the restaurant far below them. He did care for the innocent people who might be hurt or killed. He threaded his way up toward the gondola operator. To his left, Frost could see they were approaching one of the supporting trestles. Slipping the "liberated" Woodsman from under his coat, he nestled the muzzle of the silencer against the operator's ear.

The young man started to turn toward him and Frost simply said, "Don't!"

"What do you—" the man started to say in heavily accented English.

"Shut up—stop the lift by that trestle there up ahead, then lock the control panel and hand me the keys. Be quick about it!" Frost glanced over his shoulder. If any of the gondola passengers were aware of what he was doing, they concealed it well.

But all that changed as the gondola lurched awkwardly to its mid-air stop. With the cutoff of the power as the operator locked the panel into the power off position, the wind outside the gondola was deathly audible, the gondola swaying pendulum-like over the open gorge beneath them. There was a scream from one of the older women passengers and two of the younger men started toward Frost. He brandished the gun and the men settled back.

Forcing a smile, Frost said, "Would you believe I'm hijacking this to Cuba?"

Nobody laughed. Shrugging his shoulders, Frost turned to the lift operator, saying, "All right, jack down that ladder—I'm going up top. Move!"

The operator jumped at Frost's command, reached up to the heavy steel ladder at the roof of the car and released the securing brackets at the base and halfway up the sides moving the ladder down in place. "Now climb up there, open the hatch and move back down and away from it."

The operator, hesitantly at first until Frost brandished the pistol once again, climbed the ladder, wrestled the metal handle on the Plexiglas hatch and pushed at the panel. "The panel, she's stuck, Mr."

Frost glared up at the man, "Then push harder!"

"It's the ice, Mr."

"This is the gun, Mr." Frost said, faking an imitation of the young man's heavily accented English.

The boy pushed harder, Frost turning to watch the ever advancing gondola behind them. Frost looked back as he heard the cracking sound of the ice breaking away, then felt the cold rush of air as the hatch was thrown open. Gesturing with the gun, he followed the boy with his eyes as he carefully climbed down the escape ladder, then stepped back along the far side of the gondola beside the rest of the passengers.

26

Keeping his gunhand free and pistol leveled, Frost climbed the ladder, boosting himself the last few feet onto the roof, his legs still dangling inside. The trestle was an arm's reach away. Carefully, the roof of the gondola slick with wind-polished ice, he pushed himself to his knees, then tossing the keys inside to operate the gondola, Frost edged toward the trestle. Already below him, he could hear the operator shouting to the passengers to hang on. Frost knew what the boy was planning and had to beat him. As Frost stretched out his left hand for the trestle, the gondola below him lurched suddenly. Frost's timing had been off. He dove forward, grasping for the trestle supports as the gondola literally flew from under him. Hanging by his left hand, some fifty feet above the snow, Frost rammed the silenced Woodsman pistol into his trouser band under his ski jacket. Already, his left hand was freezing from contact of exposed skin to below-freezing temperature metal.

The pain excruciating, Frost struggled his ski glove onto his right hand, then swung that hand onto the metal trestle framework, getting his feet onto the supports and taking the pressure off his left hand. If he tried to move the hand he'd leave the skin from the palm of his hand behind. Edging up the trestle until his left hand was even with his belt line, Frost removed the right glove again, supporting himself against the trestle with his knees and the damaged left hand.

He pulled down the zipper on his fly, reached his right hand inside his pants and drew his penis free, then urinated on the frozen-to-metal left hand. The heat of the urine temporarily warmed the metal surface sufficiently so that Frost could free the hand without losing his skin—it was an old trick used by Arctic Explorers and presumably taught to them by the Eskimos.

Hooking his right elbow on the trestle, he pulled the glove back on, then worked his way down the trestle, the gondola carrying the three gunmen already within firing range. Frost dropped the last few feet into the snow, bathed the injured hand there, then slipped his glove over it. The gondola was nearly above him.

Without skis, he was helpless for any protracted race across the slopes. Frantically, his eye searched the terrain surrounding him for a good spot for a fight against the three assassins. There was a stand of pines off toward his left and he started toward it across the snow. Already, he could hear the gentle plops of the silenced pistols firing from behind him. Slipping, sliding, falling through the snow, Frost reached the stand of pines, dove for cover behind a deadfall and wheeled his own silenced Woodsman toward the three gunmen. Two of the men were firing from their stalled gondola while the third man was climbing down the trestle, as Frost himself had done moments earlier.

Frost thumbed the frame-mounted safety into the off position, squared the Woodsman's front sight into the rear notch and squeezed. Accurate sighting was hard with the muzzle-heavy silencer, but his shot was good, the man on the trestle loosening his handhold and grasping at his left kidney, then collapsing backward and falling like a stone into the snow. Frost feigned movement from his crouching sprawl behind the deadfall pines, the gunman closest to the roof line of the gondola reaching up and making to fire.

Frost wheeled, firing the Woodsman pistol two-handed and connected twice on the second gunman, his first shot entering the man's throat, the second slamming into the forehead above the right eye. The gunman fell back at an unnatural angle, his legs still wedged inside the gondola, his torso swaying back and forth outside the gondola like a palm tree in a strong wind.

There was one more gunman. Frost could see the ski-masked man gesturing with his pistol to the gondola operator, the operator frantically moving his hands over the panel. The gondola started speeding away. Frost's lips drew into a bitter snarl—there was no hope the meager .22 would penetrate the Plexiglas of the gondola. Lurching through the snow, Frost took his one gamble—the first gunman. His pistol hadn't looked like a .22. Frost's hands almost flew through the snow beside the body, then he moved the body itself. The gun was a Walther P-38K 9mm with a Walther silencer attached.

The smile-frown lines creased his face and Frost leveled the pistol toward the gondola, gambling the automatic was still functional. He fired a fast two-round burst, the high speed 9mm Parabellums shattering the Plexiglas near where the gunman stood, the gondola now some forty yards from him. As the gunman leveled his pistol to return fire, Frost fired once, then once again.

Fifty yards away now, Frost could see the man crash back against the opposite side of the gondola. The gondola lurched and the gunman plopped forward toward the shattered Plexiglas, his face a bloody mask as he ripped away his toque, then slumped out of sight, the glass where his face had touched it covered with blood.

Chapter Two

Frost's feet and hands were cold, the left foot particularly, stiff and feeling as though perhaps it were frozen, but ahead of him as he rolled down the embankment, the moonlight giving an almost bluish appearance to the snow, he could see the lights of the town. He rolled back the cuff of the storm sleeve on his ski jacket—the luminous black face of the Omega read almost eleven. Against his better judgment, Frost had ditched the Walther and the silenced Woodsman back along the trail.

He had no idea what sort of reception committee might be waiting, but since the law was one of the candidates and both pistols were nearly empty and he'd found no spare ammo, the guns wouldn't have been that much of an advantage in any event.

As he entered the edge of the town, the snow here on the road well beaten down making for easier walking except for its slipperiness, there were few people in the streets. Sounds of disco music were coming from some sort of lodge at the opposite end of the street and he walked toward it. He could barely feel any of his extremities now. He passed a thermometer and glanced at it—translating from centigrade to Fahrenheit, the temperature, roughly, was twenty below zero and there was a strong wind, although what little exposed skin he had could barely sense that anymore.

He stopped at the end of the street, an 1890's style streetlight illuminating the icy steps of the lodge from where the disco music was coming. Swaying on his stiff feet, Frost dragged himself forward and up the wooden steps. It took him a good minute to manipulate the fingers of his right hand to where he could grasp the door handle and depress the latch, but finally he got it right and pulled open the door. There was a second door just a few feet farther ahead, but already, out of the wind, the air seemed warmer to him.

He had an easier time with the second door, getting the hand-finger combination sorted out much faster, then pulled the door toward him.

The disco music seemed to be blaring now, and

as he staggered onto the carpeted floor of the entrance hall, he pulled his ski mask away, his eyepatch coming off with it. He walked forward. A woman in a floor-length, expensive-looking glittery formal stared at him—he could tell she was looking at the scar where his left eye should have been. She raised her hand to her mouth, but didn't scream, simply stepped back toward the edge of the carpeted hall, flattening herself against the wall there, jarring a small, ornamental framed mirror, her shoulder bumping against it and making it sag at a bizarre angle.

Frost walked past the frightened woman, stopped beside the maitre 'd's podium-style desk, then took another step forward. The heat of the sweating bodies on the dance floor, the lights—Frost's head was starting to swim. He missed the first step past the desk and started to fall. There were screams as he toppled down the half dozen or so steps and he wanted to tell them all to be quiet—he couldn't hear the music when everyone was screaming like that.

Frost opened his eye. As he started to raise his right hand to his aching head, he could feel his eyepatch clutched there in his fingers. And the fingers moved. They tingled a little, but as he looked at them they weren't blue-black and gangrenous from freezing. He started to sit up. As he moved his legs—the legs and toes worked too, he realized happily—suddenly he was very dizzy and he lay back. He opened his eye again—there was a concrete ceiling perhaps eight feet above his head. He looked down toward his feet. Perhaps a yard beyond the end of the cot on which he lay was a heavy chainlink grating. As he moved his head to follow the grating he saw that the barrier extended from one concrete wall to the other.

"Shit," he said, muttering the word under his breath.

"What is it that you said, American?" a voice asked, heavily accented with the German tongue—like the boy who had operated the lift.

Frost pushed himself up on his left elbow and looked past the steel grating—a uniformed police officer sat at a bare table, an American girlie magazine in his left hand. "What, do you want another sheet for your bed?"

"No," Frost groaned, sitting up and wishing he hadn't. "Not sheet—shit. German word I think is scheiss," then turning and smiling at the man, he added, "you know, like sheisskopf—well, we'd say shithead."

The man nodded, then looked back to the magazine. Frost searched his pockets, found his cigarettes but the Zippo lighter was gone.

"Hey," Frost said, "got a light, pal?"

The policeman turned, looked back at him, shrugged his shoulders and tossed the magazine, open to the centerfold, onto the table, stood up and walked toward the cell. "Here," the man said, "keep them, I don't think you will burn yourself," and he handed Frost a box of matches.

Frost nodded, lighting his cigarette, pocketed the matches and turned toward the back of the cell a moment, putting his eyepatch in place. When he turned toward the grating again, the policeman was still standing there. "I know it is not any of my affair, American, but how did you come to injure your eye so?"

"What?" Frost said, his face creasing into a smile, "The eyepatch—how'd I get it?"

"Yah, how did you get it?"

Frost leaned back against the cell wall, then bending his head against the grating his voice almost conspiratorial-sounding, said, "Well, it's not much of a story really. But I did make a great deal of money after I sued the shirt manufacturer. You see, I was about to be married—that was years ago. It was going to be a formal wedding—all the bride's relatives had been invited, all my friends from my days in the proud service of my country— the glorious old U.S. of A. But at any event, I went out and bought a tuxedo. Nothing fancy—in fact it was a close-out, the old shawl-collar style. My bride helped me pick it out. Well, at least she was going to be my bride before tragedy struck. It was the day of the ceremony. Claudelia—that was her name, Claudelia—well, she looked like a vision— the wedding dress was covered with lace. Ah . . ." Frost sighed. "But, as we stood there before the minister and she was about to say I do I was just so excited—there she was the girl of my dreams. It was an outdoor ceremony—we both loved the out-of-doors—she was that kind of a girl. Well, it started raining. Since we were almost through with the ceremony, we decided to go on anyway.

35

Just as the minister was about to pronounce us man and wife, the rain intensified. My shirt collar was soaking wet, and I could barely breathe. Suddenly, my collar button popped off right into the minister's face. I turned toward Claudelia and that's when the horrible thing happened. My defective shirt collar had shrunk so suddenly in the rain there that as I turned around, my left eye just popped right out of my head into the middle of her bouquet. Well, I'm sure you can guess the rest. They rushed me to the hospital and eventually I recovered, but Claudelia had been so shocked by the whole affair that her psychiatrist said she had developed a pathological fear of men wearing shirts. Joined a nudist colony not long after that. Last I heard she was coming along well until her new love strangled himself one morning when he was going to town and decided to wear a turtleneck sweater—Poor Claudelia," Frost sighed.

He looked at the cop. The man looked at him, his brows knit into an expression of puzzlement and said, "This is all true, American?"

"Oh, yeah," Frost said, nodding his head. "No sheiss." Frost stubbed out his cigarette and lit another. As he started to turn back to the policeman, the door beyond the table at the far side of the room opened and the cop, moving faster than Frost would have thought he could, ran to the table and stuffed the girlie magazine under his uniform jacket. Through the door came a second policeman and a man, very American-looking, wearing a business suit under a trenchcoat. The

36

man spoke with both officers in German for a moment, then both of the policemen left.

Frost stood leaning against the grating, just watching. Still standing in the middle of the room, the man turned to Frost and said, "Well, Captain Frost. Looks as though you were pretty busy up there on the mountainside. My name's Halston—I'm with U.S. State Department security."

He approached the cell and held up an I.D. card that looked impressive enough. Frost said, "I'd invite you in, but, ah . . ." then gestured toward the grating between them.

"Yeah, I know," the man said, sighing. "You're a lucky man, Frost. You fell into a real mess back there on the mountain, but if you play your cards right you'll come out of it smellin' like a rose, pal."

Frost let his right wrist go limp for a moment, smiled and said, "I like gardenias better." Stubbing out his cigarette on the floor of the cell, Frost walked away from the grating, turned back and said. "You tell me—just what happened back there on the mountain?"

"Come on Frost, cut the jokes. Everybody knows you stumbled onto a political assassination, killed four men and a woman and severely damaged a cable car. They could get you for kidnapping if they wanted to, but I'm here to bail you out—if you cooperate."

"What, I kill a bunch of your boys—contract agents for the Company or something?"

"I wouldn't have any idea what you're talking

about," the State Department man said. "The man who was killed was Miguel Aguillara-Garcia. He was the number two man in the military junta ruling Monte Azul—small Latin American country."

"Yeah," Frost said, "I heard of it."

"Although the U.S. government certainly doesn't condone many of the actions of the junta, Monte Azul is considered a friendly nation and our government would have nothing to do with causing one of its leaders any harm."

"Yeah, well death is sure about as harmful as you can get, isn't it?" Frost said, looking intently at the man.

"What, you trying out a new nightclub act or somethin'?"

"Oh, yeah, I open in Vegas right after this place—110 years from Tuesday. Hope you can make it."

"That's my point, man, for God's sake let me finish."

Shaking his head, then lighting a cigarette, Frost muttered, "Go ahead—yeah."

"Fine, Aguillara-Garcia was here in Switzerland for two purposes—he was consummating an arms deal and he was just about to look you up. He'd set up the meeting near here so he could contact you immediately afterward."

"Why me—what? Was he hiring people?"

"Monte Azul has a big terrorist problem—really big," the State Department man said. Hooking a chair with his left foot, he pulled it beside the grating in front of Frost's cell, then straddled the chair. "He was buying arms, frankly, because we won't give Monte Azul anything until the government softens up and restores some civil rights down there. And he wanted you, we understand, because things have gotten so bad that the junta doesn't really feel it can trust anyone. Aguillara wanted to employ you to hire a small mercenary force to act as the palace guard, the security people to guard Aguillara's brother—the President of Monte Azul, General Phillipe Mendoza Aguillara-Garcia."

"Weren't you guys sort of cutting off your noses to spite your face—that arms embargo thing? Monte Azul is the strategic key to Mexico and the Caribbean for Castro's Commie friends."

The State Department man said, "Monte Azul may be strategically important, or at least considered so by some, but any nation which indulges itself in summary execution of suspected terrorists cannot be encouraged. However, unofficially of course, we do support the principle of Monte Azul protecting itself, and of course we have no desire to see any harm come to any of Monte Azul's officials—even though they weren't elected. That's why we'd like you to take that job bodyguarding President Aguillara-Garcia. As the death of his brother the general has amply dramatized, he certainly appears to need protection."

"What's the catch?" Frost asked.

"Catch? None really," the man said. "In fact, you will be paid $35,000 to take the job—we consider it that important. And, to make sure things get done properly, we will hand-pick the dozen mercenaries you will be asked to provide. That $35,000 is in addition, of course, to whatever monies you and the government of Monte Azul agree upon. We've taken the liberty of making a few discreet inquiries, Captain, and your finances are nothing to write home about. Add to that the difficulties I'm sure you can imagine we'll have in order to secure your release—well, you can see that we'd appreciate your cooperation in this small matter. You see," the State Department man said, pausing a moment for dramatic effect, "while you are in Monte Azul there exists the possibility that your government might require your services for another—totally unrelated, mind you—situation, in the event it should arise."

"I'm not smoking somebody who hires me, especially somebody who's anti-Communist. You can leave me here to rot if that's what you want."

"Now listen, Frost, your State Department would never ask any citizen to do anything like that."

"Bullshit," Frost said emphatically.

"Seriously, Captain Frost—totally unrelated matter which may or may not arise—all I can say is that it would be a security function requiring trained personnel who could be trusted—likely no violence would even be necessary. Certainly nothing like you're suggesting. Now," the man said deliberately, "do I get the man to turn the key or do I leave?"

Frost looked at him a moment, then said, "Get him to bring my cigarette lighter and knife too, huh?" Frost lit a cigarette then with the match box and left it on the small railing against the grating blocking the cell—for the next guy, he thought.

Chapter Three

The jet engines warming up near him were imposssibly loud, the noise level heightened, at least seemingly so, by the clearness of the cold air that early in the morning as Frost stood on the runway in the international section of the Zurich airport. He watched as the plain gray casket of President Aguillara-Garcia's dead brother was put aboard the aircraft. Once the baggage superintendent nodded to him that all was secure, Frost, hunching up his shoulders under the lined raincoat he wore, started forward toward the passenger stairs. Shivering, he almost welcomed the prospect of disembarking thousands of miles south, near the sweltering tropics in Monte Azul.

Frost walked up the steps and followed the stewardess to his seat, handing her his raincoat which she stowed in the carry-on compartment above him. His flight bag and suitcase were already stowed with the luggage, his metalifed Browning High Power 9mm there as well.

As the engines increased in volume, the hatch sealed, the plane jockeying into position for takeoff, Frost settled back. He had gone to the Mexican Embassy in Zurich to officially express his condolences on the death of the distinguished citizen from Monte Azul—the Mexicans handled diplomatic affairs for the smaller country in all but the most major capitols. Later that day, Frost had been contacted to return to the Mexican Embassy and take a personal call from President Aguillara-Garcia, inviting Frost to accompany the President's brother's body to Monte Azul where Frost could be personally congratulated for eliminating the unfortunate man's assassins. Frost, of course, agreed. He'd been able to pry little more from the State Department man—officially the U.S. Government knew nothing about the identity of the assassins, but unofficially assumed they were likely hired by the Castro inspired terrorists in Monte Azul. Frost decided to dismiss the entire problem for the moment—he was tired, and now more than ever the idea of the sunlit warmth of Monte Azul seemed appealing, for as he started to close his eye and sleep, his mind drifted back to the

43

cold slopes where he'd come perilously close to frostbite and death—frostbite. As he shifted position in the window seat to get more comfortable and sleep began to wash over him, the word seemed so amusing to him—Frost-bite . . .

Frost didn't awaken for at least an hour, the stewardess rousing him and offering lunch. He ate heartily and drank sparingly. By the time he arrived in Monte Azul it still would be early morning because of the time difference and there would be a full day ahead of him.

He took a magazine in Spanish and forced himself to read it—he hadn't spoken the language for months and felt he'd be a bit rusty. Trying to get through the contents page confirmed that for him. Later, he slept again.

Not hungry when he awoke, he passed up another snack that was offered him, had another drink and leafed through the Spanish periodical again to kill the remaining hour before landing. As the pilot brought the plane around for the last pass toward the airfield in the capitol city of Monte Azul, Frost could see heavily armed troops swarming across the field in jeeps and two and one-half ton trucks, and as the plane touched down, the wheels skidding, the engines throttling back, Frost could see sparklingly polished black Cadillac limousines driving onto the field as well, armed motorcycle troops surrounding them. And, at the end of the caravan, was a hearse.

As the jet drew to a halt before the troops, the rest of the passengers aboard the aircraft noticeably alarmed, the plane's captain came on the speaker system. "Ladies and gentlemen, there will be a very slight delay for normal departure. We have been honored to carry aboard this flight the coffin containing the body of an important official in the Monte Azul government. This coffin will be removed by the military honor guard you may have noticed on the airfield to our port side. Also, one of our passengers, a Captain Frost, instrumental in bringing the assassins of the deceased official to justice, will disembark here as well for the presentation of an award from the President and fine people of Monte Azul. Thank you." The announcement was repeated in Spanish as Frost loosened his seatbelt. Obviously, the pilot had been reading a prepared speech transmitted to him by air traffic control before landing—the language was too carefully chosen for anything else.

As Frost stood up, the stewardess rushing toward him to get his raincoat from the carry-on compartment, all eyes in the first class cabin turned to him, as if to say, "So you're the guy who arrested the killers!" Frost smiled at the thought. Arrested nothing! He'd killed four men and a woman, and primarily just to save his own skin.

As Frost walked down the aisle toward the opening passenger hatch, a little boy sitting on the end seat tugged at the bottom of his sportcoat. Frost stopped, the stewardess behind him almost piling into him. "Hey, mister," the boy said. "Why are you wearing an eye patch? Are you

45

a pirate?"

The little boy's mother started to try shutting him up. Frost leaned down to the boy, eyed the all-day sucker in the boy's sticky-looking glistening right fist and smiled. "Well, no son, I'm not a pirate. Actually, when I was a little boy just like you, I was eating a big sucker—just like the one you've got there in your little hand. There was just a little bit left on the sucker, too. That was in the days of wooden sticks, though." Then, touching the boy's shoulder with exaggerated tenderness and glancing toward the budding corpulence of the boy's mother, he went on, "Well, I'm sure you can imagine the rest. I just wolfed down that sucker so fast that I started getting the hiccups—that stick from the sucker just went right into my—well, I don't want to frighten you." Frost smiled and patted the boy on the shoulder, rose to his full height and walked on, chuckling.

"What about my baggage?" Frost said to the stewardess as he reached the hatch and she handed him his coat.

"That's already been arranged for, sir," she answered. Walking through the hatch, Frost supposed he had expected blazing hot sun, but it was raining, suddenly and heavily. He slipped his arms into the raincoat and almost immediately began to perspire as he walked down the passenger stairway—the coat still had the lining in place that he had shivered with back in Zurich.

Unphased by the downpour, the military honor guard waiting at the base of the staircase and flanking a waterstaining red carpet, brought their M-16s to Present Arms. As Frost reached the midway point on the staircase he stopped a moment, noticing the meticulously uniformed general officer coming down between the ranks to meet him, a younger, less spectacularly decorated officer walking discreetly a half pace behind and to the general officer's left.

As Frost reached the base of the steps, the General stopped, came to potbellied attention and saluted Frost, saying, the English quite good but heavily accented, "Capitan Frost, our nation is honored, sir."

Feeling rather stupid since he wasn't wearing a uniform, Frost snapped himself to attention and saluted anyway. Apparently, he thought, it was the right thing to do—the General seemed to positively beam. Automatically it appeared, the troops fell into ranks behind them as Frost followed the General back along the squishy wet red carpet and across the field toward a waiting limousine. The younger officer made to shelter Frost with an umbrella, but Frost waved him away—he was already soaked to the skin and the cooling effect of the rain almost felt good to him.

Frost followed the General into the back seat of the huge Cadillac, the younger officer behind him holding the door then entering the front seat. Seated in a jump seat facing rearward, Frost wiped the rain from his face with his hand and looked up. Across from him sat three people—a man in the middle of the seat, more spectacularly uniformed in dress blue than even the General had been; to the man's right a very attractive red-haired woman in her late thirties or early forties; and to the man's left a fresh, beautiful raven-haired girl barely in her twenties.

"Capitan Frost, both as my country's President and merely as a man who deeply mourns the personal loss of his brother, let me both welcome you to Monte Azul and convey the deepest gratitude—" and at that the General, or President—Frost was temporarily unsure of how to address him—offered his hand and Frost took it, the handshake surprisingly warm despite the rehearsed formality of the greeting.

"Thank you, sir, for your graciousness," Frost said. "My only regret is that I was unable to prevent your brother's unfortunate death. I know the deaths of his murderers must be small comfort to you, sir."

"Si, this is true, but at question here," the President said, "is the bravery with which you comported yourself. I was given the full details by the Mexican Embassy and also by your own State Department. You are, sir, and always will be, a hero to the people of Monte Azul, and I will personally be forever in your debt. Please accept this small token of the affection our nation feels for you and our appreciation of your bravery."

The sodden General who'd saluted Frost by the passenger staircase handed the President a long black velvet box. The President opened it and took from inside it a medal similar in appearance to a

48

Victoria Cross. "I bestow upon you, Capitan, the highest decoration of the government of Monte Azul—the Cross of Valor, you would call it." And, as the President leaned forward with outstretched hands to Frost, Frost bent toward him and the President placed the medal around his neck. "We cannot salute, Capitan, because of course we are both seated. But the greatest salute between men is in the heart, no?"

Frost nodded, smiling, and feeling a little ridiculous at the same time. "Now, Capitan," the President went on, "if you would honor us to be our personal guest at the funeral of my brother— God curse this rain, but the heavens are no doubt weeping for the loss."

"No doubt," Frost muttered, the remark seemingly unheard as the President nodded to the General beside Frost and the General tapped the chauffeur—also in uniform—as a signal to proceed. Behind them, Frost could see the loaded hearse, festooned with elaborate floral arrangements even in the driving rain. Slowly, the movement of the great car in which they rode almost imperceptible, Frost watched through the window as the funeral procession assembled, the motorcycles taking up formation around the caravan. Then the cars began picking up speed and crossing the airport runway, through the chainlink fence gates, moving out onto the highway. As they proceeded and Frost longed for a cigarette but could see no ashtray, he observed that the rain-driven road was devoid of any traffic other than the high-speed procession of which he was a part. Flanking the road on both sides were widely spaced jeeps and motorcycles, each with an armed man at the controls, and each in turn falling in behind the motorcade as it passed.

By the time the caravan turned off the main highway and onto a mud-rutted red clay road leading up toward the mountains, Frost thought the funeral procession had more the appearance of a military convoy.

They traveled the unpaved road for only a few minutes, then turned off onto a better kept gravel road, this only a car's width wide. After a moment, the vehicles stopped, then began to move again, only more slowly. As they passed between iron grillwork gates, Frost looked through the window. Rounding a curve on the road Frost could observe a small pickup truck—Japanese apparently—driving ahead of the forwardmost motorcycle—leading them he guessed to the cemetery plot.

The rain was still coming down hard as the caravan gradually drew to a stop, a military honor guard assembling outside the black limousine in which Frost rode with the President and First Family. The President gestured politely and Frost stepped first out of the car, the young officer already waiting in the rain, holding the door.

As Frost snapped up the collar of his soaked through raincoat—this time no one offering him an umbrella—he stepped forward. As the President, the woman Frost assumed to be the President's wife and then his daughter exited the vehicle, following the equally wet General, the young officer raised a large umbrella, a second officer running forward with another to cover the First Lady and her daughter.

Frost let them pass him, then fell in beside the General and walked up the hillside along still another red carpet, already soaked through, toward the deep purple canopy covering the grave site. A Catholic priest, already beside the neat rectangular hole, came forward to shake the President's hand.

The bulk of the military force was waiting, Frost surmised, outside the cemetery, only the original motorcycle escort standing near the graveside, apparently ready for a rifle salute to the fallen brother of the President.

As the service began, Frost looked around, surveying his company. There were some thirty troops in all from the motorcycle patrol—Army blue dress uniforms immaculate but rainsoaked, white gloves, combat boots with intricately patterned white lacing up the front, white helm—he stopped. The motorcycle trooper third closest to the President—Frost stared at him, their gazes meeting and the trooper looking away.

There was something about the soldier. As a background to his thoughts he could hear the droning of the priest's voice as he prayed over the coffin. The combat boots, Frost thought—something was wrong with them.

Suddenly, Frost was distracted. The priest had stopped speaking, the young officer who had accompanied the General called the motorcycle troops to attention and directed them to raise their M-16s preparatory to firing the salute. A bugler struck up something vaguely reminiscent of a cavalry charge, the instrument sounding a little flat—Frost had played a bugle in a corps once in one of the military academies he'd attended. If memory served him, it seemed to be that the mouthpiece of the bugle was more difficult to control in a heavy rain. As the soldiers shouldered their rifles, preparatory to firing, Frost, at attention beside the General, glanced back to the trooper whose appearance had somehow bothered him. As he did, he saw the muzzle of the trooper's M-16 waver, then suddenly sweep downward toward President Aguillara-Garcia.

Frost tried to remember the Spanish words for "Look out," but they wouldn't come to him. There was time for only one thing, he knew. Frost threw himself forward toward the trooper, his left hand slapping the muzzle of the M-16 upward, his right knee smashing toward the soldier's groin. The M-16 fired, full auto, the bullets smashing savagely through the canvas canopy covering the grave.

Frost's right knee connected and the trooper started to fall back, his right hand though still clutching the assault rifle's pistol grip. Frost took a half step forward, released the rifle and crashed his left elbow down toward the soldier's jaw, then drove his right fist in a straight arm karate blow aimed at his adversary's Adam's apple, crushing his windpipe. Frost ripped the M-16 free as the trooper fell back, already dead, into the open grave of the brother of the President whom he had just tried to assassinate.

Before Frost knew it, troops were swarming over him and as he started to shout, Frost could hear the calm voice of President Aguillara-Garcia saying, "Release that man, fools, he alone saved my life."

And a second later, the President was beside Frost, personally extending his hand to help Frost to his feet out of the mud. "How did you know that man wanted to shoot me, Capitan Frost?" the President said, breathless.

"Look down at his boots—everybody else had a ladder pattern in the white bootlaces—his were just laced the normal way." The bottom of the grave was already three inches deep in water, ground runoff that half obscured the dead assassin's face.

"You tried to save the life of my brother," the President said, "and you have saved my own life, perhaps the lives of many others. My brother had wanted to hire you to lead a team of men you yourself would select, a group of professional men at arms, such as yourself, men to protect my own life and the lives of my wife and daughter. What you have done now goes to prove that my brother had indeed chosen the right man. Will you stay and help us, Capitan Frost—these terrorists, Madre Dios!"

"Si, el Presidente, esta bien," Frost said.

President Aguillara-Garcia merely nodded. Wet, the bottoms of his uniform trouser legs mud-splattered now, the President walked back to his brother's coffin, removed his hat and there, standing alone under the edge of the protective canopy, the man dropped to his knees in the mud, his hands clenched in prayer on the coffin lid.

Frost turned around and looked away. The rain hadn't let up. The romantic in him could rationalize that very easily.

Chapter Four

Frost had sat alone at the table for thirteen in the seaside Miami motel's restaurant for only ten minutes when the first three men arrived—Jake Fledgette, Carl Bilstein and Deke Craymer. Rather than starting in with only three men there, Frost ordered drinks for everyone (Fledgette ordered a Shirley Temple just to upset the waiter). In less than a half hour, Carrington, Pete Shoerdell, Kilner, Nifkawitz, Sturmer, Barrington, Pearblossom, Riddel and Santarelli had arrived as well. Pearblossom, Riddel and Santarelli had arrived together and since Frost had never worked with either of the three, he felt he should have known them since their references were so impeccable, he pegged them as the State Department ringers—the rest of the men had been recruited for him by an undercover State Department man, so Frost had no reason to trust any of them—and he didn't.

After the waiter finally came with the last of the drinks and refills for Frost and the early arrivals, Nifkawitz said, "So just executive protection—civies, the whole routine?"

"Pretty much so, it's a paramilitary operation," Frost said, staring into his rum and coke, "but that's the basic thrust of the thing—babysit the President, his wife and daughter."

"I'll take the daughter," Sturmer said, his fair-complected cheeks ruddy-looking under the overhead lamp, his blond hair almost orange in the light.

"Yeah," Pearblossom said, "Yeah, I'll bet you'll take the daughter."

"Okay, if it will calm everybody down I'll take the daughter," Nifkawitz said.

"The point is, guys, this is gonna be no picnic," Frost said. "That sucker I killed at the funeral was well infiltrated—half the army could be with the terrorists for all I know or anyone else knows. That's why the President's hiring us."

"Everything—no charges for ammo, food, anything?"

"Yeah, everything's paid for—including funeral expenses," Frost said, laughing then, most of the men laughing as well. "We leave tomorrow, just like you were told. So, any questions, or you guys just wanna stop all this screwin' around and eat?"

"Hell," Deke Craymer said, "I can eat down there—let's drink."

Frost chewed an ice cube a moment longer, then said, "Hell if that doesn't sound good to me. Hey," he shouted, "hey waiter!"

Already, Frost was waving his finger around the table and signaling for refills.

The chartered aircraft, twin props revving, waited on the tarmac. Frost, for a change using the dark glasses just to avoid the glare, wore his best rumpled white suit, a black silk knit tie at half mast under the open collar of his white shirt—his face was stubbled gray and black since he'd skipped shaving that morning and he scratched at his chin.

It was Nifkawitz, standing with Frost and the others while the remaining baggage was stowed in the cargo compartment aboard, who asked, "Hey, Frost, how'd you get the eyepatch?"

Rubbing his right temple and wishing he'd drunk less the previous night and early that morning, Frost looked behind him, his hands on his hips, then rasped, "Well, now I tell ya, Nifkawitz. It's not such a big thing. Actually, it's really not much of a—" Shaking his head then and wishing he hadn't, Frost fished a rumpled Camel from his pocket and balled the pack in his right fist. "Hell—" He said nothing more and just walked toward the plane.

Chapter Five

"Capitan Frost?"

"Yes, ma'am," Frost said, turning in mid-stride as he walked down the main floor hallway of the Presidential Palace.

"I am so comforted, Capitan, by the presence of you—and your men, too, of course."

Frost just stared at the First Lady a moment, saying then, "Thank you, Senora. I'm pleased that you feel that way."

Smiling and starting to turn away, he heard her voice behind him say, "And would you like to have even a greater honor bestowed upon you, Capitan, Capitan with the one eye and the body with all the scars. I watched you swimming last night after you and your men settled in. You have a fine body and many scars. Have you fought over women a great deal, my Capitan?"

"Not over them so much, Senora—I was usually too busy any time I was over one." As he started to turn away, he felt her hand touching the sleeve of his coat.

"Am I not attractive to you, Capitan—Hank?"

"Oh," he said, smiling at her, "certainly you are ma'am, sure thing. Listen, though, Senora, I gotta go make everything secure now. Watch your husband, all that good stuff, you know."

"No, Hank, but you can tell me if you must. I like to hear your voice—what you Americans call a whiskey voice, too much of the whiskey and cigarettes."

"You're perfectly right, Senora, fella like me shouldn't even be permitted to talk to a lady like you."

"I permit you," she whispered. "I will permit you a great deal more."

Frost looked over his shoulder, lit a cigarette from his half empty pack of Camels and replaced his battered Zippo in his jacket pocket. "Senora, look. What about your husband?"

"Capitan, your loyalty—such devotion. My husband," she whispered, pressing her body against him, pulling at the lapel of his white suit, "he is very kind to me, like a father to me in so many ways."

Frost sighed hard.

"But my husband, Hank, he would kill you if I told him we were lovers, how you forced me to take you into my bed. Oh, how I tried to resist! But if you happen to feel otherwise, then I will tell him nothing—and after all, you are in charge of security, no?"

"If I don't make love with you, you tell him I did and I get shot, right?"

"Correcto, Hank."

"And if I do, you don't tell him anything and I don't get shot, si?"

"Si, es claro, no."

"Oh, si, es muy claro. Como se dice, your bed or mine, doll?"

She smiled, Frost didn't and she leaned up, whispering in his ear, "Mine, I have a certain place."

I bet you do, Frost thought and as he followed her down the hallway he thought he caught a glimpse of Marina, the President's daughter, watching from the farthest doorway. But then he turned and caught up with La Senora Anna Aguillara-Garcia Ruiz, her round little behind in the tight black sheath she wore beckoning to him. As he started up the steps after her, she turned to him and said, "Oh, and, Hank, there is one thing you must know."

"Yeah," he said, cocking his right eyebrow at her, the Camel burning out in the left corner of his mouth.

"What I most seek in a man younger than my dear and respected husband is ardor, la passione.

We have three hours before you can even expect my husband to return from General Commacho's briefing at Army Headquarters. I want you to drive me insane with passion all that time, es claro?"

Frost started looking for an ashtray for the cigarette butt—it had died in his lips. He just held it in his hand. "Yeah," he answered, reaching out and taking her offered right hand roughly in his own a moment. "Even to a guy with one eye, you're real clear."

He walked beside her up the stairs. He didn't see a single servant. He guessed she had planned well in advance. Following her into her room in darkness, he half expected her to have whips and chains on her walls, but when she drew the drapes 'a moment and sunlight filtered in he saw none of that. He saw a forty-year-old nymphomaniac struggling down a zipper on a too tight dress that hid a body he assumed was probably still pretty terrific, a body she'd probably blackmailed other men with before, a body under other circumstances he might not have disliked at all.

"Take off you clothes, Hank, and come to bed— now, my Capitan."

He looked down at her as she stretched across the bed like a big lazy cat. He looked down into his hand—he still had the cigarette butt in it. He tossed it into the ashtray beside the small couch near the window, then stripped off his coat. He was wearing the Browning High Power in a diagonal carry JerryRig shoulder holster he picked up in Miami. He stripped the JerryRig off and put it on the seat of a fragile-looking oriental

61

lacquered chair, then kicking off his shoes walked over to the bed.

"You always carry a gun, do you not, Capitan?"

"Siempre, si." And Frost, leaving the Gerber knife clipped inside his trousers, took them off and dropped them on the floor beside the bed, pulled off his shirt and shorts and socks and lay down beside her.

"Diga me, Capitan, do you like my body?" she asked, quietly, almost subdued.

Frost leaned over toward her, his left arm circling under her neck, his right hand moving to touch the nipple of her left breast. "I'll tell you later, okay?"

Frost didn't wait for an answer. The fingers of his left hand entwined into the hair at the nape of her neck, his right hand moving down to the small of her back, his arms drawing her body up to him, her head cocked back, her lips moist, parted and, oddly Frost thought, slightly trembling. He brought his mouth down on hers, the tips of their tongues touching. Frost could feel a shiver move up her spine. Their legs entwined and his fingers found the delta of hair at her crotch, then found their way inside her, to the moistness already there.

Frost could feel her hands searching and feeling his shoulders, his back, touching his chest, the tips of her fingers almost teasingly touching the nipples of his own breasts. Already, he was fully erect, and he found his way inside of her, felt her body writhing under him, her small muscles expanding and contracting around him, her pelvis rising, falling, then rising again. After an indeterminate time there was an explosion that both of them made and felt and as she collapsed into his arms, Frost shot a glance down to the black face of his wristwatch. Two hours and ten minutes at least before he could count on the President to return . . .

As Frost stepped from the doorway of the First Lady's private apartment and into the second floor hallway in the West Wing, he pulled the knit tie up, not bothering to button the shirt collar, then ran the fingers of his left hand through his almost black hair to push it back from his forehead. Closing the door, he shrugged his shoulders and reached under his coat to get the JerryRig holster with the Pachmayr gripped Browning High Power where it belonged. As he reached the edge of the hallway and started down the stairs, he stopped—the voice stopped him, the voice the pleasant sounding alto of Marina, the President's daughter by his first marriage. "You look like an unmade bed, Senor Frost, did you enjoy my stepmother's favors?"

Frost turned and looked back up the steps at her. "If you know where I was then you know why I was there, don't you?"

"You are a mercenary, no?"

"That's what they call me."

"And you have just made love to the wife of your employer, no?" she said.

"Sex is a better word for it—made sex, not love."

"Then," she said, "you are both a murderer and a traitor. How can my father trust such a man as you?"

"Let me tell you something, missy—and hear it good. I came down here to keep your father alive, and that's just what I intend to do. Now if his wife gets me shot, I won't be able to do that, will I? Or if I have to get out of the country to avoid your father's wrath, I still won't be able to keep him alive. If you're so God-awful holier than thou and so damned concerned about your father, then mind your damned business and let me keep him alive. Once he's dead," Frost said, his voice low since he heard the voice of President Aguillara-Garcia in the main hallway, "she'd never be able to cheat on him, would she?"

"Eho de p—"

"Tsk, tsk," Frost said, "such language. Wash your mouth with soap," and he turned his back on her and walked down the rest of the flight of steps and into the main hallway.

"Ah, Capitan Frost! All goes well, my friend?" President Aguillara-Garcia said, seeing Frost at the base of the steps.

"Si, el Presidente, at least as well as can be expected," Frost remarked.

Chapter Six

"We must go, Capitan Frost. I have been characterized in the press very often as a military dictator, and I am, but only because I care for the welfare of my people and cannot trust a democratically elected regime to quell the Communist terrorist movement. And the people of the province of Playa Sur have been victimized so terribly by the terrorists that their economy is in ruins, perhaps hundreds of children have lost at least one parent, dozens both parents. The people there are being helped—we are sending trucks with food, medical supplies. But that is not enough. They need to know that their leader cares. I must go, and as head of my personal security staff, it is your job to get me there. We are both military men, my friend," President Aguillara-Garcia said, "and I realize the tactical problems such a trip will represent to you, but it is unavoidable. But at least I leave the arrangements for the trip in your hands—to hopefully make the task more manageable."

By now, having spent more than a month in the country and most of it close by the President's side, Frost knew that to argue was hopeless. The terrorists wanted Aguillara-Garcia dead, at whatever the manpower cost necessary to achieve their end. And Aguillara-Garcia, military dictator though he was, characterized himself well—he was a man deeply concerned about his people and their welfare, more deeply than most of the citizens of Monte Azul would ever realize. There would be no stopping the man from traveling into the hotbed area of terrorist activity, making public appearances, walking through the streets, shaking hands with the people, stopping to wipe the nose of a crying child or help a peasant woman lift a heavy load. Frost almost wished the man were a tyrant—tyrants were easier to protect.

"Pero, el Presidente," Frost tried in Spanish, then giving up said, beginning again, "But Mr. President, you've heard the old line before—if an assassin is sufficiently dedicated, dedicated enough to die and these men are, there is no possible way, regardless of the precautions I take, to guarantee your safety—no matter how skillfully we plan, no matter how hard we try."

"I know that, amigo, and if the unfortunate does occur, then it is fate, and it will not be you who must take the blame, but me, for I have chosen to thrust myself into the situation and you—you are only trying to make the best of it." The President lit one of his thin cigars, then said, "These are from Spain, you know. I would never smoke a Cuban cigar until Castro is no longer breathing. You will plan my route? I wish to leave the morning following tomorrow."

"Si," Frost sighed, "si, el Presidente." And Frost turned and walked from the room. He walked down to the end of the first floor hallway, less than a dozen steps from the President's main office, and entered the guard room. Three of his mercenary force were on duty there—Fledgette, Bilstein and Craymer—and all three turned and looked to the door as he walked in. Frost moved to the table occupying the center of the large room, on it the weapons he had ordered for use by the security team. He took little comfort, despite their excellence, in these tools of his trade finally being available to him—weapons alone would not save President Aguillara-Garcia.

"This is good stuff, Frost," Craymer, one of the two blacks in twelve men Frost had hired said.

"Tell me about it, yeah." Frost picked up the Steyr-Mannlicher SSG .308 Win. caliber sniper rifle, the green synthetic stock not the most eye-appealing thing in the world, but the gun one of the most accurate sniper rifles ever devised. With the Kahles scope mounted to it, it was as close as possible to the perfect, out-of-the-box rifle. There were six MAC-10 .45 ACP caliber submachine guns, with suppressors and spare thirty-round magazines, the full auto, not civilian legal pistol versions. These and specially customized CAR-16 selective fire telescoping stock assault rifles completed the shipment. Frost wondered really how much of an advantage the specialized equipment would be, since even after a month of working together he still didn't trust the men he'd hired to use it.

The rest of that afternoon was spent in consultation with General Commacho, the man who'd met him at the airport in the rain when he'd first arrived that day, and the one member of the ruling military junta headed by President Aguillara-Garcia that Frost and the President both seemed to trust. With Commacho's help, Frost planned the route, the support aircraft to be used and several diversionary troop movements to keep the terrorists hopping, hopefully in the wrong direction, away from the President.

Frost begged out of his scheduled meeting with Anna, the First Lady, using the legitimate excuse that he needed to get to sleep early since he would be up and moving by four in the morning. Frost retired for the evening by 9 P.M. and could not sleep, neither could he relax.

Perhaps the thing he regretted most since the

loss of his left eye years earlier was the more rapid eye-strain he developed in his right eye, when reading. Before the incident had taken place, he had always read voraciously. Now, despite the perfect vision in the right eye, it still strained more easily and caused headaches. Naked, he got up off the bed and walked over to the full-length mirror on the far wall, stripped away the eyepatch and stared at his face. The lines in his cheeks were deep, lines that hollowed into furrows when he smiled or frowned. The drooping dark mustache drew his face out even more. Late at night, especially after shaving well before 6 A.M. as he had that day, the stubble of his beard showed up considerably, gray in the cheeks and under the chin, the gray of his sideburns seeming to increase each time he saw his reflection. And there was the scar where the left eye had been. He'd always told himself the patch was something he wore for other people, rather than himself. But as he stared at the scar, recalling the myriad jokes he'd told over the years instead of the truth about the loss of his eye, he wondered. He remembered the time Bess had seen the scar, kissed him and sincerely, he felt, not been— The word he was searching for, he wouldn't say. As he walked back to the bed and lay down, turning off the light and starting to at last drift off to sleep, he silently wondered where the real scar was . . .

The horizon showed no evidence of the sunrise yet as Frost peeled out of bed, dropped to the floor and did the customary fifty pushups—customary unless the previous night had included too much drinking, and this one hadn't. He shaved with an electric razor, preferring it when he was somewhere where there was electricity. He showered, washed his hair and dressed, making a mental note to brush his teeth after he caught some breakfast. He walked quickly and quietly down the deserted second floor hallway and down the back stairs to the kitchen. The staff would already be up since the President was planning to be on the road by seven himself and would be awake in another hour.

Frost sat at the small table farthest away from the stove after pouring himself a cup of steaming hot coffee and finding milk to cool it with. As the old woman who was the chief cook walked into the massive blue-tiled kitchen and saw him, she nodded, muttering something about "Americanos" and without even asking got out three eggs and a small steak, then set about slicing a potato. While the food was cooking she brought him a full carafe of coffee and a small pitcher of milk to drink with it, then a glass and pitcher of orange juice she'd freshly squeezed. Still muttering under her breath but saying nothing to him, moments later she brought him the food she had cooked and bread fresh from the oven with a bowl of whipped butter. Figuring he'd be exercising a lot that day anyway, he ate his fill and after finishing a fifth cup of coffee, flashed the woman a smile, muttered "Gracias, mama," and went back to his room.

Frost brushed and flossed his teeth, then checked the High Power once again, wiped the Metallified chrome finish with a dry rag, then reinserted the pistol in the diagonal JerryRig holster. He checked the Gerber MkI knife—it too was as it should be.

Grabbing the Safariland black nylon "SWAT" bag he already had packed, he left his room and walked down past the Presidential office and entered the security room. It was just past six—Carrington, Shoerdell and Kilner were just coming on duty.

"Howdy," Kilner drawled.

"Yeah," Frost muttered. "Mark it out for me—I'm drawing one of the CAR-16s and six twenty-round magazines—anybody comes by, I'll meet 'em outside."

"Right."

Frost said nothing more, he felt like saying nothing more. He had never worked with men to whom he had felt more distant in all his life. Even in the combat zones of Viet Nam, or later after the loss of his eye in the combat zones of inner city high schools as a teacher, or later still in all the mercenary armies he'd traveled with in Africa and Latin America. He lit a cigarette and stood on the front steps of the Presidential palace, the Colt assault rifle under his left arm. Loosening his tie a little more, hunching his shoulders against the damp cool of the predawn morning, he leaned against one of the antebellum South style squared pillars and waited.

Glancing down to his watch, then looking back at the unbroken horizon he could see it—the near-white brilliance, the sun rising . . .

There was a certain thickness almost to the sound of the rotor blades whirring in the humid

71

mid-morning air, the helicopter's sliding doors open, Frost and six of his mercenaries riding with the President and General Commacho in the center helicopter. Commacho had resisted the idea of the President suffering the ride without air conditioning, but the President had forced Commacho to bow to Frost's wishes. "If the doorway must be opened for Capitan Frost to feel he can do his job properly, then why should I resist? I have not come here for my personal comfort—I have come here to comfort my people. And I cannot do that if Capitan Frost is unable to do his job of preserving my life."

Beneath, Frost saw as he scanned the ground they covered, was a seeming unbroken jungle, an occasional rise of ground, then more of the jungle itself. Craning his neck as the helicopter climbed to pass over a low mountain range, he could see the coastline and the breaking white caps of the ocean far beyond.

Forcing himself, he drew his eye away from the seaside vista fast coming up before them and back to the ground. The 45-minute helicopter ride had gone too smoothly—he knew something or someone had to be waiting. Smiling almost bitterly, he saw it—the flash of glass from the jungle before them. Perhaps a scope on a sniper rifle, perhaps an optical sight on a rocket launcher, he wasn't sure. He disliked ordering indiscriminate killing, but in this case there was no choice.

Frost shouted to the six mercenary soldiers behind him, saying, "Down there, twenty degrees or so left off the nose—hit it heavy!" Then as the men moved toward the open door of the chopper, the Steyr-Mannlicher SSG, two Colt CAR-16s and three MAC-10s sweeping over the ground below and poised to fire, Frost yelled forward to the helicopter pilot—"Give me a hard forty-five degrees to port, then zigzag back 45 to starboard; keep it up until I tell ya' different."

As the helicopter started banking left, the shooters by the open portside doors leaned into the fuselage to keep from falling to the ground, and started firing. Already, from the ground below them as the black shadow of the helicopter flashed over the bright green tree cover, Frost could see the whisp of smoke, the trail of a rocket. He watched, almost spellbound, the din of gunfire around him meaningless to him, the rocket reaching out for him and for all the lives in the helicopter, then almost miraculously passing. Apparently a switch-hitter time delay and/or impact fuse, the rocket exploded in mid-air fifty yards beyond them. Snatching up his own rifle, Frost joined his six men by the open door and fired down into the target zone. There were no more rockets forthcoming and after another moment or so of evasive action Frost shouted to the helicopter pilot to resume his normal flight pattern, but move up another thousand feet or so. As the chopper climbed, Frost looked back into the killing ground behind them—the jungle, at least from the air, was for all intents and purposes undisturbed. The violence and possible—likely—death of the anonymous person behind the rocket launcher seemed almost absorbed, forgotten as soon as it occurred.

He breathed a sigh of relief. Now that something had happened, something he could cope with and counteract, he somehow felt more at ease.

The helicopters crossed over the final mountain range and followed the seacoast northward toward San Luis, the capitol and only major city in Playa Sur province. As the Presidential helicopter circled the city, the other three support helicopters close around it, Frost assessed the area. Half the houses—shanties was a more appropriate term—looked wholly uninhabitable, destroyed by fires and bombings of the terrorists. The bulk of housing seemed to be along the wharves of the city itself, a shanty the size of a large outhouse, some half-rotted looking boards that were part of the dock, then a fishing boat tied out front. As the helicopters swung in low over San Luis, the children on the streets below ran out of the houses and waved—probably their parents had told them to, Frost thought. Perfunctorily, he waved back. Soldiers always wave at kids he remembered—sometimes the kids threw grenades or had explosives taped around their chest. One of the many thrills of terrorist warfare. After thousands of years of armies fighting other armies around the globe, from primitive tribes to conquering Romans to "civilized times" someone had finally found a way to make children an active part of warfare instead of just its victims. Sometimes the inventiveness of humankind, Frost thought, made one feel like throwing up.

As first the guard helicopters landed, then the

Presidential chopper inside the rough circle they formed on the edge of town, fifty or more armed men from the San Luis garrison raced into the circle at double time, M-16s held at high port. Before Frost was able to set foot outside of the Presidential helicopter, the soldiers had already formed a ring around it, three men deep. A portion of the ring opened and a well-uniformed officer— by now Frost could recognize the rank designation, this man a full Colonel—passed through, attended by two aides marching discreetly behind him. Frost smiled, laughing to himself. Even General Commacho, Commander of the Army, only had one aide, and usually he kept the young officer too busy to even be with him— as was the case this trip.

The Colonel stopped, ignoring Frost, snapping to attention as first General Commacho and then President Aguillara-Garcia exited the helicopter. Frost listened to the words exchanged, watched the smiles, but didn't even bother to mentally translate the conversation—it was likely the same drivel high ranking officials usually threw at one another, he guessed.

Frost heard his name mentioned, shook the offered hand of the Colonel and, as the Colonel tried encircling President Aguillara-Garcia with his own men, Frost stepped in between. The Colonel took a step back, then glared at Frost. "Permitta me, por favor. Habla Ingles, Colonel."

"Si, un poco."

"Muy bien. I guard the President, got me?"

The Colonel glared at him still. Over the

Colonel's shoulder, Frost could see Commacho's face, the smiling corners of his mouth revealing his slight amusement. Frost stared at the Colonel; the Colonel continued staring back. Frost said, "I got half as many eyes, but I bet I can stare twice as long."

Frost glanced to his left; the President's hand was clamped onto his shoulder. "My friend, I have known Colonel Sanchez for years—we both attended Academy together. Come with us please, but you can trust Colonel Sanchez as I do." Frost breathed deeply, looked around and back at Sanchez, then looking down to button his sport-coat, said, "Si, el Presidente, a sus ordines."

Sanchez had plans, Frost could clearly see that, and now he paid close attention to the conversation between the President and the Colonel. Sanchez wanted Aguillara-Garcia to come to his villa and rest, Aguillara-Garcia wanted to see the terrorist devastation close at hand—and immediately. After some talk and Sanchez trying to convince Aguillara-Garcia otherwise, the Colonel did the inevitable and bowed to his President's wishes.

After five minutes of waiting—Aguillara-Garcia preferred to stand in the street a hundred yards away from the now quiet helicopters—they began the tour of the city. Walking a step behind Aguillara-Garcia and weaving from one flank to the other, Frost kept his CAR-16 slung across his right shoulder, right fist on the pistol grip, trigger finger just touching the edge of the guard, safety lever set to full automatic. He'd left two of his mercenaries to stay with the guards on the helicopters—these Commacho's men whom Frost somewhat trusted. The other four mercenaries Frost had interspersed in the circle of military personnel around the President.

It took just a matter of a few minutes to walk down toward the wharf area and the collapsing houses a few feet from the boats tied there along the dock. There were several children in front of the first house, bellies swollen with hunger, deep circles under their eyes.

Aguillara-Garcia pushed his way past the guards surrounding him and went over to the oldest child—perhaps eight, though far too small for the age—and knelt beside her. In Spanish, he said, "What is your name, girl." She answered, "Stella" but because of the language the word was pronounced "E-stella." "When was the last time you ate your fill, child?" Aguillara-Garcia asked. Stella didn't remember.

Aguillara-Garcia looked up at the Colonel, saying, "Where is the food I have been sending?"

"There are administrative problems, my chief," Sanchez said, noticeably uncomfortable.

"Your combat troops, they have rations, no?"

"Yes, President."

"Assemble your men—immediately."

Sanchez looked noticeably more uncomfortable, but turned and rasped a short command to a subordinate, the man taking off at a run back along the way they had come. Aguillara-Garcia stayed crouched beside the child, on one knee with her there in the mud abutting the wharf, then said

77

to the little girl, "I want you to find every child you can and bring them all here to me—you know who I am."

Although he hadn't posed it as a question, the child's face brightened and she said, "You are our President."

Aguillara-Garcia smiled, saying "Yes, daughter, I am. Now go, quickly."

The child started to run off, then Frost noticed her limp—the left leg was terribly crooked, probably from rickets as an infant.

Frost watched Aguillara-Garcia as he in turn watched the disappearing little girl. She was smart, Frost thought—she was starting at the last house in the row first. Children, already more than a dozen, were starting to pour out of the end houses and come down the street, some running, some walking timidly, all in as bad physical shape as the little girl. As Frost watched the army of starving children start to assemble, he suddenly felt something odd, the feeling you read about but slightly disbelieve in books, the sixth sense that causes the small hairs on the back of the neck to hackle up, like a voice telling you, "Beware!" Frost turned and looked behind him. There was a small boat with an outboard engine coming up alongside the wharf, drifting, apparently no one aboard. But there was a canvas tarp neatly spread over the entire inside from gunwale to gunwale.

Frost took a step back, shielding President Aguillara-Garcia with his body. As he did, the hump under the tarp in the boat started to move— a man coming to his knees with a submachine gun in his fists. As the gunner aboard the boat started to open up, Frost shouted to the men around him to get down, then pivoted toward the gunner and twitched his finger against the CAR-16's trigger, loosing a three-shot burst toward the assassin, then another, then still another. The machine gun was still going off, the trail of the gun ripping across the brakish looking green water.

As Frost kept up firing, the soldiers around him began firing as well, Sanchez making the first shot with his pistol, the men under his command following his cue. The submachine gun fell limply from the hands of the man aboard the boat, his body already collapsed in a bullet-riddled heap. Everyone was still firing. Frost, grammatical Spanish failing him, shouted, "Alto—alto la fuega," roughly, "Stop the firing."

Everyone was staring at him then, and Frost, ramming a fresh twenty-round magazine up the well of the CAR-16, turned back to look at Aguillara-Garcia. "Esta bien, amigo," the President said. "Once again, I owe you my life."

"We'd better get the hell out of here, Mr. President," Frost said, looking down at the hand Aguillara-Garcia had, for the second time that day, on his shoulder.

"I have business here, this is why I came." And Frost turned, the children now—perhaps fifty of them—huddled in a knot of fear halfway back along the wharf.

Aguillara-Garcia rose to his feet, then smiling and bending forward called to the children. Sanchez started to intervene, Frost bringing the

CAR-16 to port and blocking his way. "Colonel, like I said before," Frost said icily, "I guard the President—comprende?"

Sanchez turned and walked through the wall of troops and disappeared.

The rest of the day in San Luis was without incident—Aguillara-Garcia toured the town house-to-house, doing what he could of an immediate nature to help. And by the end of that day, Frost could well see Colonel Sanchez was in terrible trouble—Aguillara-Garcia making it perfectly clear that Sanchez had not distributed supplies and foodstuffs as directed. A scam, Frost wondered, but he wasn't sure—political corruption wasn't his department. Throughout the day, small portions of the Sanchez's force had disappeared, units being called away, perhaps joining Sanchez himself. Throughout the day too, Frost got a growing feeling of discomfort.

As the day wore on, Aguillara-Garcia and all in his company working through customary lunchtime without stop, Frost substituted two of his mercs to personally guard the President and found General Commacho, then walked with him for a while, Frost discussing his feelings regarding Sanchez. Surprisingly, Commacho agreed—he too was getting a growing feeling of distrust for Sanchez, despite the friendship Sanchez openly expressed for Aguillara-Garcia. "Colonel Sanchez is not acting like himself—my men and I, that is why we have not been with you. We have been investigating the reserves of supplies. Aside from the immediate needs of the troops garrisoned here,

80

there are no supplies—nothing."

"I don't understand," Frost said, lighting a cigarette and stopping beside one of the helicopters.

"It is mysterious to me as well, Capitan Frost. Sanchez is a rich man, richer by far than El Presidente or myself. There would be absolutely no need to steal supplies or sell them off."

"Fortunes change, General. Perhaps Colonel Sanchez is no longer so well-heeled."

"Heeled, he was not sick?"

"No, I don't mean it that way. Well-heeled—an American expression for being well set up financially—do you follow my meaning?"

"Si, yes, but I know Sanchez well—he is still as you say, well-shoed. He loaned the government the equivalent of a half million yankee dollars six months ago, and not less than a month ago, offered to make more funds available, which we did not need. We had already repaid the half million. No, there is something less obvious here."

"I don't want Aguillara-Garcia at the reception tonight," Frost said.

"You cannot prevent it, mi amigo. No es possible. But, we can certainly heighten our vigilance, be doubly on guard."

"The terrorists—do you think he's working with them?"

"Sanchez? That is impossible to imagine," Commacho said, decisively.

"Then what other explanation, look at the terrorist activity in his province. Look at the missing supplies. Those are good looking troops

81

Sanchez has. If he's half the man you say he is, he shouldn't be having the problems he is. And then that assassination attempt today from the boat."

"Yes?"

"Why did Sanchez take so long to 'arrange' things for El Presidente to tour the docks, why the delay? And why didn't any of his troops open fire on that submachine gunner until Sanchez himself fired, after I'd already killed the man and eliminated the threat?"

"You ask questions for which I have no answers, amigo. Have you told these thoughts to El Presidente?" Commacho lit a thin cigar, then stared back down the street into the town, searching out the sunset, Frost thought.

"Hell, I haven't been able to get his ear at all. He's a good man, Aguillara-Garcia—none of this is phoney, false, I mean. He is genuinely concerned for these people. You look at his uniform?"

"Si."

"Both knees are covered with mud from when he's knelt down beside children, to talk to them. He's already stripped Sanchez's men of their field rations and he's demanding more. He may have something planned for Sanchez tonight himself."

"We must all be ready, amigo. What do you suggest?" Commacho sculpted the tip of his cigar against the edge of an exposed strut on the nearest chopper.

"I want every one of your men inside the Colonel's headquarters, as near to Aguillara-Garcia as possible. All but two of them. Those two and two of my security people I want outside, hidden, in direct radio contact with you and with me, to alert us to any sort of attack in force."

Commacho fell silent for a moment, then said, "If it will not be possible to trust the men under Colonel Sanchez, I doubt we will do well against a massive terrorist assault. We may be walking into a trap. I will also guard the helicopters too I think."

"You can't," Frost said. "We don't have enough men, not nearly enough. If El Presidente insists on dining with Sanchez, confronting him there, we will be too far from the helicopters to reach them if fighting breaks out, and there are not enough men to guard El Presidente and these machines. We have no choice."

"You are right, of course, my friend," Commacho said, his voice tinged with more than a trace of bitterness.

Frost and Commacho started off together, back toward President Aguillara-Garcia, then splitting up, Commacho to arrange for the troop placement for that night, Frost to resume his vigil over the President. He found himself liking Aguillara-Garcia a great deal, and more importantly respecting the man, his determination only stronger that he would not let the man die.

By nightfall, Aguillara-Garcia was visibly exhausted, having been on his feet for close to ten hours, his breathing short, his cheeks flushed. Meeting with Commacho again for a moment, Frost drew the General aside, whispering, "Why didn't anyone tell me El Presidente has a heart condition?"

"It is not something, of course, which we like to make known. He pushes himself too hard—he always has," Commacho answered. Then, "All is ready with my men. When do you think it may occur—the attack?"

"I don't know. If they're smart they'll either hit just as we enter Sanchez's headquarters or once the dinner has begun—see if you can chisel me a sandwich now that I think of it."

"What is this chisel—a rock sandwich? Surely you joke, amigo."

Frost looked at Commacho. "I'm the one with the bad jokes, remember? No rock sandwich—I meant see if you can sneak one to me. I'm starving."

"Si," and Commacho left.

To get to Colonel Sanchez's residence and headquarters it was necessary to walk the length of the city—less than half a mile—down the main road. Commacho wanted to send a man ahead for a car or jeep, but Aguillara-Garcia had squelched the idea. Frost guessed El Presidente had the same suspicions Frost himself held and wasn't about to send some unsuspecting soldier into Sanchez's stronghold to get murdered. Aguillara-Garcia walked, Frost ignoring protocol and this time a few steps ahead of him, the four remaining mercenary guards and Commacho's men, save for the two on perimeter guard with Frost's other two mercenaries, surrounding the President.

No one occupied the houses flanking them along the dusty road they walked—it was too dangerous to live close to the military headquarters because of the terrorist activity. All houses there abandoned, a few boarded up. It was a perfect spot for an ambush. Frost had no way to counter it either. If he divided his forces sufficiently to check each house along the way he would have nowhere near the strength needed to guard the President if an attack broke out.

The road curved slightly, just before reaching the headquarters and as Frost and the Presidential guard rounded the curve, all automatically stopped. In front of them, across the road and blocking it, were some fifty men from Colonel Sanchez's force, Sanchez himself at their head. There were heavy machineguns mounted on bipods, at least a dozen men with submachine guns, the rest of the force armed with M-16s.

Frost started to speak, felt Aguillara-Garcia's hand at his shoulder and stepped aside, reluctantly, as the President pushed past him, moved a few paces forward, then shouted, "So, my old friend! This is the game you play. But why?"

Sanchez said nothing for a moment, then apparently not to be outdone by Aguillara-Garcia, stepped a few paces ahead of his men and shouted, "You must surrender. My men block you here, others are in the buildings along both your flanks, there are men behind you. You will not be harmed; I have been promised this."

"Then indeed you are not only deceitful, but you are a fool," Aguillara-Garcia shouted back. "Why, I know, but I wish to hear it from your own lips, my old friend."

Frost shot a glance to Commacho, the General

only nodding back to him and signaling with a palms downward motion for Frost to be patient.

"There is good reason, El Presidente," Sanchez shouted. "You have betrayed the people."

"In which terrorist manifesto did you read that, Sanchez?" Aguillara-Garcia asked calmly. Frost stared at him. The President was tall and straight, the direct physical opposite of the portly, somewhat short Commacho, but like Commacho dark of hair and eye and with more than a little gray at the temples.

"I will not carry on this absurd conversation—you must surrender."

"Oh, must I, old friend. I think not, Sanchez." Frost looked back at Commacho—in Commacho's left hand was a small radio transmitter. Looking more closely in the semidarkness there, Frost thought he could see the push to talk button depressed. Frost turned back to listen to Aguillara-Garcia. "I learned the tragedy of your son, Colonel. I knew what you were doing here, but I chose not to act until I verified it with my own eyes." A smile crossed Frost's lips, despite the seeming inevitability of impending death—he wished he could say 'with his own *eyes*.'

"What do you mean, the tragedy of my son?" Sanchez said, the timbre of his voice belying the boldness of his words.

"He was captured by the terrorists and you were made to do their bidding in the vain hope of them sparing his life. You have not heard from him for several weeks, I know. If you were to be able to deliver me, you were promised his return. And as a man who is still your friend, despite all this, it grieves me to be forced to tell you—we found his body four days ago. Your son Manuel is dead, and hideously so, amigo."

"You lie! You lie," Sanchez repeated over and over.

"Believe me, I wish that were so," Aguillara-Garcia shouted back. "It is I now who must ask you to surrender, Colonel Sanchez—Pedro, I ask as a friend. I do not want your death."

Frost watched Sanchez, he watched as the inevitable happened, and somehow Frost sensed Aguillara-Garcia had known its inevitability ever since he had planned the trip to the coastal province, that Aguillara-Garcia and Commacho had troops waiting, waiting for the confrontation Aguillara-Garcia and Commacho had known would come and that he, Frost, had not been told because they had known he would not have allowed the President to so risk his life.

Frost turned to Commacho, flashed his biggest, toothiest, phoniest grin and rasped, "Thanks, thanks a lot—nothing like openness to cement a friendship." Not smiling, Commacho shrugged back. Frost looked down to Commacho's hands, the General's holster empty of the .38 Super Government Model Colt he habitually wore, the right hand slightly behind his back. The left hand still held the transmitter, but the thumb of the hand was frantically pushing and releasing the talk button, opening and closing the frequency, a crude but usually effective means of signaling someone monitoring the same band. Frost looked back to Commacho's face, raising his eyebrows quizzically, catching Commacho's eyes. The General nodded and moved his right hand from behind his back, showing Frost needlessly the gun he held, the hammer already cocked.

Frost glanced back toward Sanchez and his troops, less than twenty-five yards away from them—point-blank range for assault rifles and machineguns. His right hand tightened on the pistol grip on the CAR-16, his finger edging inside the trigger guard and against the smooth, revolver style trigger. He drew his left hand up to his necktie and pulled the tie further down, opening another button on his shirt. As he started to bring his left hand down, he eyed Sanchez. Sanchez was starting to turn, to step back toward his men. In the distance, on the night air, Frost thought he could hear the whirring sound of helicopter blades—he hoped, almost prayed, he could hear them. Sanchez looked up, shouted "Lo sciento, El Presidente," as loud, apparently, as he could and swiftly swept down his right hand—a clear signal to open fire.

Before Sanchez's hand finished its downward arc, Frost leaped in front of the President—behind him, Frost could hear the booming of Commacho's .38 Super, but then the general gunfire from all sides was too loud and strong to hear anything else. As Frost reached Aguillara-Garcia, his left hand ripped the Browning High Power awkwardly from his shoulder rig, the hammer thumbing back, the CAR-16 now blazing from his right hand, the 9mm pistol spitting 115-grain gilding metal-jacketed hollow points from his left. Frost elbowed Aguillara-Garcia down to the ground and dropped beside him, on both knees, firing still.

He heard the boom of a pistol shot, glanced toward the President and saw him, propped on both elbows in a prone position, firing an engraved, stubby-barreled Colt Python .357 Magnum revolver, the high polished blue of the gun showing like a mirror with each flash from the short muzzle.

Thinking, "Dammit, he's incorrigible," Frost went on firing. His pistol shot dry first and he dropped it to the ground, then fired a last burst from the CAR-16, swapped the magazine there and loosed a burst as he fished an extra magazine from the clip dump under his right arm, thumbed open the snap there and then grabbed at his Browning. Still firing the CAR-16, he used his left index finger on the release button on the 9mm pistol, dumped the spent magazine and rammed the new one up the butt bracing it against his kneecap. He worked the slide release down and got the gun firmly into his left hand, then started firing again with it.

Around him, like flies in an insecticide fog, Aguillara-Garcia's troops were dropping, their wedge between the President and the gunfire now coming at them from all sides, thinning them almost sickeningly. At the top of his lungs so someone could hear him, Frost shouted, "General Commacho—let's hit that closest house—move," then grabbing at Aguillara-Garcia, getting the

President up and onto his feet as best as he could, Frost started running, the Browning rammed into his trouser band now, the CAR-16 with one of the last of his fresh magazines, spitting 5.56mm fire at any target of opportunity.

Frost could see Aguillara-Garcia from the corner of his right eye, going into a classic FBI-style crouch to stop and fire his Python. Once, Frost roughly grabbed Aguillara-Garcia by the shoulder and pulled him along. An old war horse, Frost thought, his respect for the man increasing. They reached the nearest house, Frost breaking through the doorway first, at least six heavily armed terrorists with AK-47s inside. Frost sprayed the room, Commacho and Aguillara-Garcia right behind him now with a half dozen troops, shooting into the terrorists until even their bodies stopped twitching with death.

Frost kicked aside a terrorist slumped by one of the shot-through windows and snatched up the AK-47 beside the dead man, then started emptying it toward the Sanchez position.

"Where the hell are those choppers, Commacho?" Frost shouted.

"They are coming, amigo."

Frost glanced beside him as he reached down and grabbed another AK, his shot empty. There was Aguillara-Garcia, the little revolver still in his hand. Frost gave up, it was pointless to try to keep Aguillara-Garcia in relative safety—the man was too much of a fighter. Frost turned back to the open window. Sanchez's troops were storming toward the house. A few loyal troops were still in the street, and Frost had caught sight of his four mercenaries and a handful of the surviving Commacho troops heading into the next house beside them, but that was all that was remaining. The street outside was littered with the bodies of Commacho's men.

Commacho, his Colt .38 Super in his right hand, was talking frantically into the radio held in the other. The Spanish was so comparatively rapid Frost could barely understand every third word. Then, turning and looking toward Frost, his face positively beaming, Commacho shouted, in English, "They can see the house. They will be on the ground in less than two minutes—Madre de Dios!"

As Frost turned back toward the window, he could hear the rotor blades clearly now over the gunfire, see the Sanchez forces starting to turn back. And he could see Sanchez himself running back toward the headquarters. As Frost turned toward Aguillara-Garcia, the President was stiffly getting back to his feet, starting for the door. Frost grabbed the President's arm. "Where are you going?"

"To do what must be done, my friend—and you cannot stop me."

"Sure," Frost said, "who the hell listens to me—I'm just your bodyguard. Where are you going?"

It was Commacho who spoke. "To kill Sanchez, amigo. What else can a man do?"

"Ohh," Frost said, nodding his head in disbelief. "He could have a dozen men in there with him."

"He will not, amigo," Aguillara-Garcia said, then turned and strode through the doorway. The street outside, by comparison to a few moments earlier, was as quiet as a cemetery. The fighting still raged on, but was spread across the town and in the surrounding vegetable fields to the west.

"Hell," Frost said, despairingly. Then, gesturing to Commacho, Frost and the men from the house followed after Aguillara-Garcia, laying down fire as needed as the President marched, seemingly oblivious to the gunfire, toward the villa where Sanchez hid.

Frost changed sticks for the last time with his CAR-16 as they reached the gates opening onto the villa courtyard, Sanchez's headquarters. Aguillara-Garcia turned, saying, "Capitan Frost, General Commacho, my loyal friends. You may both accompany me inside, but no others. When I meet Sanchez, regardless of what happens, you are not to harm him, or in any way interfere, should he kill me I expect safe conduct for him out of the country. You both understand this?"

Frost spoke for both himself and Commacho, "Si, El Presidente." He had learned, albeit the hard way, that Aguillara-Garcia was a man of iron will, and attempting to reason with him once his mind was made up was all but impossible.

Aguillara-Garcia leading the way, Frost and Commacho stationed the six men remaining with them by the gates, instructing them to let no one inside. Frost took up the drag spot, his finger against the trigger on the CAR-16, Commacho walking almost rivetted at Aguillara-Garcia's side.

Still oblivious to danger, the President strode through the half-open doorway and into the elaborately tiled entrance hallway. "Sanchez doesn't live cheap," Frost commented to no one in particular as he glanced up at the crystal chandelier over his head. He turned as Aguillara-Garcia shouted, "Sanchez, donde esta?"

"Aqui," Frost heard from behind him, then turned, the stubby muzzle of his CAR-16 lining up on Sanchez, framed in the open double doorway leading into what appeared to be a library. Aguillara-Garcia touched his hand to the muzzle of Frost's gun to stay him. Frost moved back, up out of the crouch he'd dropped to.

Aguillara-Garcia walked toward Sanchez, then turned back to Frost. "It is as I told you, amigo—men of honor. It is between Colonel Sanchez and me—no one else."

There was a gun held limply in Sanchez's right hand, another elaborately engraved firearm like the Python Aguillara-Garcia held, only Sanchez's ordnance choice was a big N-Frame Smith & Wesson, the barrel six inches long, the hole at the muzzle unmistakably .45 caliber.

Commacho gestured to Frost and Frost followed him to the far corner of the hall. He watched as Aguillara-Garcia and Sanchez stood, motionless by the library doors. "I take it, my old friend, that you do not choose to surrender?"

"Si, but would you do me the honor of taking my life—I am a Catholic, and suicide—"

The President cut him off. "Enough said, amigo." Sanchez stepped into the library,

Aguillara-Garcia behind him, the latter's hand on Sanchez's shoulder. After a moment—a .45 from Sanchez's revolver would have made a heavier sound—there was a solitary gunshot and a little while after that, long before Aguillara-Garcia reappeared in the doorway, Frost thought he heard the heavy sounds of a man sobbing.

Chapter Seven

Chain lightning over the mountains and across the lake beside which the capitol rested, the night heavy with the rain and the wind, Frost stood inside another library, days and miles away from the place where Aguillara-Garcia had ended the life of his friend, Colonel Pedro Sanchez. Many of the terrorists had been killed that night as well, and the disloyal forces of Sanchez shot or captured. There had been executions the next morning at dawn, and Frost had stayed away. The only man he had ever shot in cold blood aside from sniping assignments in his Special Forces days in Viet Nam had been Colonel Chapmann—and that in retribution for the deaths of 250 of Frost's mercenary comrades in the slaughter in the sleepy village in South America, a village the name of which somehow he could not recall. Frost and Bess had not spoken of that assassination—but it had lived there between them all the months in Switzerland and eventually she had gone.

Both of them had known there was more for them somewhere down the road, but how far that was, neither of them could be certain. And tonight, as he watched the rain coming down, nothing to do because Aguillara-Garcia was staying the night with General Commacho as his guest, Frost's body ached for Bess. Yet at the same time he was almost deliriously happy that Anna, the President's wife, was away—Frost did not want the duty of having sex with her this night, nor ever again he felt as he thought about it. He downed the hot-in-the-throat straight whiskey from the prism bottomed glass and walked to the library bar and poured himself another drink—it was his first night off in five weeks and he was tired. It was the first waking moment in five weeks when he had not worn his gun. The romance of that amused him. He liked guns, at least mildly even after all these years of shooting, but there is nothing more tedious, he reflected, than being chained to a two- or three-pound machine with every step you take. You sweat on it, it warms against your body. After a while you don't really notice any longer that it's there, but then a telltale bump into a chair arm, a car door post—and the thought of its presence returns. You bend a certain way, you don't bend another way—regardless of the heat, like a fool you wear your coat. He had been the nine yards and back and there again. He looked at the amber-colored whiskey in his glass, felt the hotness in his cheeks—he had been there too, back in the days before he'd become someone they called a mercenary. As he raised the glass to his lips—

"Is that your vacation, Capitan Frost?"

He turned—it was Marina, Aguillara-Garcia's twenty-three-year-old daughter. "Why aren't you in bed?" he said, his voice slightly thicker than he wanted it to sound, "and that wasn't a proposition."

"It wouldn't have done you any good if it had been, Capitan—I only wanted to thank you. I haven't had the chance to see you alone since you returned from Playa Sur after fighting there to save my father. Now I have thanked you, and it is done."

"Want a glass of whiskey—I can afford to be very generous since it belongs to your father anyway!"

"So do I," she said.

"No you don't—you're too old for that. Anna belongs to him and she doesn't want to—you don't and you do. All you need is a sponsor and you guys could have an American soap opera."

She looked at Frost, then said, "How did you lose your eye, Capitan, or do you just wear that eyepatch to look mean, tough—macho?"

Frost looked around at her. Laughing, sipping

at the drink he held and trying to find his lighter, he said, "I was playing strip marble once with a bunch of cannibals—you wouldn't want the details."

She walked toward him, took a match from a stack built into the bar ashtray, struck it there and held it for his cigarette. "Being charitable to one-eyed men tonight or what?"

"You have an expression in your country—what makes you tick, Senor Frost? What kind of a name is that—Frost?"

"It's good enough for my brother Jack—what do you want?"

He watched her and after a moment she laughed. "Si—Jack Frost. You are so funny."

"Took you a minute, didn't it?" Frost remarked.

"Why do you always make the jokes?"

"What would you do if you were me?"

She thought about that for a moment, then looked out onto the veranda at the rain, then back to him and said, "I don't know if I want to answer that—do you like the rain, Senor Frost?"

"Depends whether I'm watching, marching or sleeping in it, why?"

"How do you feel about standing in it, feeling it all around you like the hands of a lover—how do you feel about that?"

"Try me," Frost said, then took her right hand in his, setting his drink on the mahogany bar. "What makes you tick?"

"You do not want to find out, Capitan."

"Hmmph," Frost grunted, then started to draw her close to him. She slipped from his grasp and went to the large French doors leading to the veranda. As he started after her, she opened them, the rain blowing inside the library in sheets. By the time he reached the doors, she was already walking out onto the veranda, the carpet under his feet as he stood there already dark with the rain blowing onto it.

Shrugging his shoulders, Frost walked out onto the veranda, following her into the rain. There was more of the chain lightning over the lake as he looked at her standing against the railing. He moved up beside her. Her hair was streaming down wet, her cheeks, her eyelashes, her lips were wet.

"Did you ever do this when you were a child, Capitan Frost?"

Frost looked at her, then put his arms around her waist and pulled her toward him. "No," he said flatly, then tipped her chin up toward his face and bent his head down, kissing her.

Marina pulled back, breathless. "I didn't mean that."

It was like something out of a 1950s movie, Frost thought. The wind blowing hard, driving the rain in sheets across the veranda, the far-off lightning, the girl there, her clothes soaked through and clinging to every curve of her young body.

Frost ran the fingers of his right hand back through his hair, pushing it away from his forehead. Then with the same hand, he sculpted the wet black hair away from Marina's face, holding her head back with his hand at the nape of her neck. The rain was hammering down on them both, her face glistening with it. "What are you going to do, Capitan—why do you look at me like this?"

Staring down at her sparkling black eyes, then brushing the rain from them with his fingertips, he drew her closer to him. She started to speak. Bending his mouth over hers, Frost rasped, "Just shut up," then crushed her lips beneath his . . .

It should have ended like that, back there on the veranda, he thought, the sun through the venetian blinds not catching him still asleep, but still making him close his eye against it. Now he was twice damned—he looked down beside him at the still sleeping figure of Marina, the President's daughter. Glancing at the watch on his wrist, he realized that in four more hours President Aguillara-Garcia and his Senora would return— Anna. And now Frost was sleeping with both Marina, the daughter, and Anna, the wife. Looking down at Marina, the darkness of her still damp hair against the eggshell whiteness of the pillowcase, her eyelids fluttering slightly as the sun now crossed them, for the moment at least Frost didn't care. He bent down and kissed her and after a second, she stretched herself almost like some little animal and without opening her eyes, entwined her arms around his neck and let him kiss her— again and again.

Chapter Eight

The terrorist bomb went off by the right wheelwell, the bullet-resistant windows of the black Cadillac limousine in which Frost rode already burnt brown from the flash of explosives as the car tipped up and rolled over, Frost diving flat across the back seat and digging his hands into the upholstery as a purchase while the car rolled and rolled and then skidded into a halt. He looked up—one of the few fire hydrants in the center of the capitol city was now a gusher.

The car was right side up. Frost leaned toward

the far door on the hydrant side and tried the handle, then when the door barely budged, he drew back and smashed at it with his left foot, the door falling away, hanging crazily on one hinge. Snatching up his CAR-16—he was almost never without it now, the terrorists' attacks having heightened dramatically since the President's successful coup against them in Playa Sur—Frost rolled out of the car. The icy cold water from the hydrant soaked him instantly as he peered over the limousine's rear deck, the muzzle of his CAR-16 close to his face.

Small arms fire was already coming at him from across the street out of a ground level shop window. As he squeezed what would have been the butt plate on a conventional rifle and telescoped out the stock of the Colt assault rifle, he glanced into the front seat—the chauffeur was dead, his head half cut from the body. Frost was silently thankful the President had not been with him— Frost was only using the President's car to visit Commacho about a security matter.

As Frost popped a three-round burst across the street toward the terrorist gunfire, he scanned the street for signs of the two-man motorcycle escort that had been accompanying him. He saw both bikes but could make out the remains of only one body. As he peered back over the trunk lid toward the terrorist position, Frost spotted the second motorcycle trooper. His helmet was gone and the left side of his face was covered with blood, but he was moving, pistol in hand, along the wall beside the terrorist position in the front of the leathergoods store. The trooper waved a hand toward Frost, but Frost could not signal back, would not risk revealing the man's position to the terrorist gunfire.

Dropping down, Frost looked across the Cadillac's undercarriage—the right front tire looked as though it might have gone flat, but he wasn't sure. Frost crept forward, toward the driver's seat. He pried open the door and it fell away. Shoving it aside, he reached across the dead chauffeur and tried the key. The big eight-cylinder engine rumbled a moment, then came to life. Pushing the chauffeur out from behind the wheel, Frost crawled inside. The steering seemed a little soft— probably a tire rod, but he wasn't sure. Already, as he slammed the gearshift into reverse, he could see the radiator bubbling and steaming—he'd bubble and steam too, he thought, if he'd just crashed into a fire hydrant.

The car steered badly, but at least it steered, he thought. He backed it away from the hydrant, then wrenched the wheel to his right as he moved the selector into drive, then stepped on the gas, the wheels straightening out as he cut diagonally across the street. The speedometer was hovering just under forty as he dove down onto the front seat, the battered, huge black Cadillac hammering through the plate glass store window into and over—he hoped—the terrorist gunmen. The car was still moving for a second after the splintering sound of shattering glass died, then it stopped like it had hit a brick wall. Rolling out of the doorless driver's side, the CAR-16 in his fists, Frost glanced toward the demolished front of the car—it had hit a brick wall. Snaking the muzzle back toward the front of the store, he spotted one terrorist dead on the floor—the car had done that. There were two more men, both with AK-47s and both still moving. Before the first man could open fire, Frost twitched the trigger on his own gun and caught the man just right to kick the bottom half of his body out from under him, the top half still going forward, the body in death dropping facedown on the floor like a rock onto the surface of a pond.

The second man was already shooting and Frost rolled across the broken glass littering the floor, came up on his knees in a low crouch and sprayed with the gun he held—no three-shot bursts—bullets hammering into his enemy's midsection. The terrorist rocked back, his AK-47 pointed up toward the shop ceiling and still firing, firing as his body careened backward and fell into a still-intact display case, shattering the glass like an explosion.

As Frost rose to his feet, the soldier with the head wound now leaning against the shattered window frame, there were already crowds of university students gathering outside. Frost went back to the rear seat of the Cadillac, took out the leather shoulder bag with the spare magazines—he didn't like it, looking too much like a man's purse—and rammed a fresh twenty-round stick into the CAR-16, then worked the bolt. He telescoped closed the stock and slung the compact .223 assault rifle under his right shoulder, his hand on the pistol grip, trigger finger just outside the guard. He walked across the broken glass toward the young trooper and stood beside him, the muzzle of his gun obliquely pointed toward the crowd of students. There had been street rioting the last two nights and Frost uncomfortably felt he was in the middle of an early start for this night's festivities.

There was a knot of three or four men in their early twenties or younger standing at the front of the crowd and Frost picked them as the ring-leaders, one in particular, taller and darker than the others—good-looking by anyone's standards.

Frost brought the muzzle of his weapon up, leveled at the young man's chest, then said, "Usted—de un paso al frente," in English meaning, "You, step forward."

The boy started toward him. "Despacio," Frost barked with his most sinister sounding Spanish accent and the man slowed down. The boy started reaching into his right pocket and Frost snapped, "Ponga los manos en la cabeza." Reluctantly, the student clasped his hands on top of his head. Reaching out to the student's shoulder with his left hand and pulling the boy toward the muzzle of his gun, Frost figured so far so good. Then aiming the muzzle of his assault rifle at the young student's head, the boy's body in front of him like a shield, Frost shouted to the others in the growing crowd, "Yo disparo si se acerca—I'll shoot if you come closer," he repeated in English.

It was a standoff. Too bad he wasn't in Mexico, Frost thought—a Mexican standoff. Somehow even his own humor didn't make him laugh.

105

"Entiende Ingles," Frost whispered to the student shielding him. "Diga me!"

"Yes," the boy said. "I understand English."

"Good," Frost said smiling. "Want to hear a joke about my eyepatch?"

There was no answer. Shrugging his shoulders and changing his tone then, Frost rasped, "I've got the selector on this thing at full auto—anybody goes for me your head's the first human Sputnik—got me?"

"Si," the student answered.

Desperately, Frost hoped the explosion and gunfire would draw police. The shield routine against the growing student crowd would only be good for another minute or two—and Frost had no desire to live up to his threat with the boy.

Already, one of the other ringleaders was starting to edge toward him. Reaching with his left hand for the JerryRig shoulder holster under his left armpit, Frost broke the thumb snap and trigger guard snap as he ripped the Browning from the leather, the hammer coming back full cock as he pointed the muzzle toward the advancing student. "Alto—Sus manos arriba—vamenos!" The boy stopped dead in his tracks, eyes fixed at the muzzle of the Browning pointed dead at his forehead, then raised his hands.

Frost had run out of hands and guns—the next guy who called his bluff would have to get shot, he realized, and then all hell would break loose. He shot a glance to the young trooper, still leaning against the frame from the plate glass window. The soldier's gun was trained against the crowd, but the bleary-eyed look he had didn't spell out that he'd be much help in a pinch.

Suddenly, just as several of the people in the front of the crowd started getting pushed forward by the growing numbers behind them, Frost heard the sirens—police! The crowd started breaking up, students running in all directions. Frost waved the muzzle of his Browning at the student he had covered with it—"Salgase de esta area." The boy nodded and ran. Frost shoved the tall one shielding him away, then pointed the muzzle of his CAR-16 at the boy, saying, "You remember, amigo—I could have but I didn't—get out of here." Like the other one, the "student radical" took off in a dead run.

As the police vans and ambulance pulled up at the half-blown away curb, the young trooper, collapsing into a heap in the glass at the base of the window frame, said, "You should have killed them both, Capitan Frost—they will be back in the streets tonight, but with guns."

"Yeah, I know—just too soft-hearted I guess." As Frost leaned down to help the trooper back to his feet and move him toward the ambulance, the boy said, "Capitan Frost—I did not know your Spanish was so excellente."

Smiling at the kid, Frost said, "It isn't—memorized a little book with Spanish phrases for police officers in it. Hell, when you want to talk romantic to a girl, though, closest thing in there was "Bend over and spread your cheeks."

It was either the joke or loss of blood, Frost figured, because the young soldier passed out.

Frost meticulously avoided Anna, the President's wife, throughout the rest of the day, but was able to snatch a few moments alone with Marina, again on the veranda outside the library where that rainy night almost two weeks earlier they had first kissed. She was wearing a dark blue, very grown-up looking long-sleeved dress, with a single strand of white pearls around her neck, her shoulder-length hair caught up at the nape of her neck in a very matronly-looking bun. "I heard about the affair this morning, Hank—thank God you are all right."

"Yeah," Frost said, taking her in his arms, "without God's providence and a little help from the Colt factory I would have been in a heck of a fix."

"Still, you are never serious."

"You try holding down my job and being serious—great way to go crackers fast."

"Kiss me, Hank," she whispered. And Frost obliged. In a moment, her lips touching his left ear, she whispered, "Must you go tonight?"

"I have to, but I'll come to you as soon as I can. I've got to see the rioting for myself so I can accurately advise your father. If we come down on the students too hard and too fast we're going to have a war, not a riot. The terrorists could just sit back then and watch the excitement."

"But," she started—

"But nothing, kid. I've gotta do my job. Otherwise, we can all hang it up. Tell you a few facts of life. You used to criticize me for being a mercenary or whatever. But right now, it seems like beside General Commacho and you, I'm the only man your father trusts. I can't let him down—it'll be bad enough when he finds out what I'm doing with you—"

She cut him off. "I think he would approve—he likes you, very much."

"Yeah, well I don't think he'd have such an egalitarian attitude toward your stepmother and me—who's he gonna believe there, his wife of seven years or some one-eyed triggerman? Uh-uh. I've gotta do what I can as fast as I can. Some night soon mamacita's gonna get sore as hell that I broke a date and find me in bed with you—then the pizza really hits the fan."

"Pizza—the fan?"

"Trouble, kid," Frost said, then taking her closer in his arms and kissing her he left her there, saying, "Tonight."

"Esta noche," she whispered softly.

The poorer part of town beyond the lake between it and the Presidential Palace had been torched before sunset, and now, although there was total darkness in the overcast sky, the street in which Frost sat in Commacho's command car was as bright as day. "Things are not going well, amigo," the portly General murmured.

"No—" Frost drawled.

"Be serious, amigo," Commacho said. "What should we do? I can order in more troops and give shoot to kill orders and the rioting will stop."

"What do you do the first time a trooper turns his back, General? Kill ten citizens for every soldier who gets a butcher knife in his kidney? If I knew what to do, I'd say it.''

"Si," Commacho said, his voice tired.

"You know," Frost said, lighting one of his Camels and popping open the ashtray from the back of the front seat, "sometimes I wish I was one of those guys in the men's adventure books—you know, taking on the crooks single-handed, fighting crackpot villains who want to dominate the earth, falling in bed with beautiful girls in every chapter—what a life! And you have the answers for every situation. All you gotta say is, 'Wait—I have a plan!'"

"Do you," Commacho said, his eyes smiling, "have a plan, amigo?"

"No, like I said, I'm not some hero in a paperback book. Maybe we can run an ad in the superspy gazette or something: 'Heroic types wanted—must supply own vintage wines and silencer.'"

"You are crazy, amigo."

Frost laughed. "You're a good judge of character. Seriously, though, the only thing I can see for us to do is contain the rioting at all cost—let 'em burn out this section of the town, then tomorrow get on the radio and take public address cars through the streets and tell them we're going to rebuild it."

Commacho sighed, "Si, we must, but then what happens tomorrow night?"

"You want me to really tell you?" Frost asked, staring away from Commacho and at the boundary of the burning houses and streets packed with armed men not a hundred yards away from their

110

staff car.

"Si, diga me."

"Okay—you can't hold on. If you had another fifteen or twenty thousand men, or if the other fifty percent of your military equipment had spare parts, you could go out into the jungle, round up the terrorists, scare hell out of 'em by giving them a fair trial and deport all the third raters, then worry about the student rioters. They'd calm down if they didn't have all the Communist terrorists feeding them all this BS about the President. If Aguillara-Garcia got to be known as a person to most of those people, they'd fall down on the ground and thank God they had him. But now all they get is Communist propaganda. But you can't do any of that."

"Then you are saying that the situation here is hopeless, amigo?"

"Yeah, I'm not saying I'm ready to give up, but I am saying it's hopeless. The best thing you could do is tell Aguillara-Garcia to get out of the country. But he wouldn't do that."

"Si," Commacho said, his voice tired, the look more of a disgusted fat man in a dead-end job than a military commander. "I know that you are right, but I could never admit that to him—I cannot. How did we lose, amigo?"

"I'm not in the sermonette business, amigo," Frost said, lighting another cigarette with the burning tip of the first one. "But I think you lost because a whole heck of a lot of the world doesn't give a damn anymore—that's what keeps fellas like me in business, didn't you know?"

111

"One thing—un otra causa, my friend," Commacho said, his face oddly brightening.

"What—would I give up?"

"Si, that is it; would you?"

"I'd get my wife and kid out of here and fight like hell." Frost snapped his cigarette out the window toward the fire line. Every house was burning, every tree was a living torch. Angry shouts filled the night.

Chapter Nine

Marina's nipples grew firm under the touch of his hands. As he bent his face to her neck, smelling the perfume of her body, Frost realized too that the smell of the fires was still on his own body. He looked up a moment, and through the half drawn drapes—the blinds were open—the flames were no less visible against the night sky, only far enough away that if you tried very hard you could forget them, pretend that the rumblings and gunshots were just odd noises of the night, forget at least, unless like Frost, you knew they weren't.

"What troubles you, carino?" Frost heard her whisper to him.

"Carino? I know that word—dear one, no?"

"More than that, Hank. What is it that troubles you?"

Frost leaned back a moment on his elbow. "How honestly do you view your father's hold on this country?"

"Very honestly—and I know the end is coming. So why do we waste our moments together?"

Sighing, nodding his head, he repeated, "'Why do we waste our moments together?' Search me, I guess," and Frost drew her over into his arms, her head resting in the crook of his right elbow. Her lips were warm, moist, like the tip of her tongue as it darted in and out of his mouth. The fingers of his right hand locked in her hair, his left hand drifted down to the small, tight rear end and held it.

He could feel her fingers playing across his back, feel the tips of her nails gently drawing an abstract there, feel them biting into him and his left hand moved away from her a moment and then found the warm opening between her thighs and the moisture there. One of her hands left his back and suddenly it was moving him into her, her pelvis rising against him, the warmth from her abdomen a burning thing. He drew her head back a moment and kissed her again, his mouth bending to kiss the nipple of her left breast . . .

The hammering at the door brought Frost awake. "Damn," was his first thought—it had to be Anna and she'd find him there with her

114

stepdaughter and tell the President. But as the pounding persisted, Frost realized it wasn't a woman doing it. As he reached for the Browning High Power beside him on the nightstand, he felt Marina stirring in his arms. "Relax," he whispered. "Just someone for me. Go to sleep."

He unlimbered his right arm from her—it was stiff. The pistol in his left hand, he walked naked to the doorway and stood beside the door jam, his voice a loud stage whisper. "Who is it?"

"It's me, Nifkawitz—let me in. Either that or come on out. Somethin' big is up and I need ya'."

"Just a second," Frost rasped, then walked back from the door and started searching the pile of clothes on the floor for his own. Her bra and his shirt had gotten tangled up and as he tried untangling them, he noticed Marina was awake.

"Go back to sleep."

"What is it, Hank?"

"One of my men—Nifkawitz. I had to tell a couple of my guys where they could find me in an emergency."

"I understand. But what is wrong?"

"If I knew that," Frost said, pulling his shirt on and then slipping the harness across his shoulders, "I'd be back in bed with you. I don't know if I'll be back tonight. If I'm not, why don't you meet me for breakfast—early before the rest of the house is up—down in the kitchen. We can make it look like a coincidence or something. Okay?"

"Si—yes."

As Frost stepped into his shoes and caught up the zipper on his fly, he leaned down across the bed and kissed her hard on the mouth, then started for the door, pulling his coat on over the shoulder holster. "Hank?"

"Yeah," he said.

"I don't know if I love you, but I want you, very much. Do not get killed."

He smiled at her, jabbing a cigarette between his lips as he did. "Right, kid—I'll put that right at the top of my list of things to do." And then Frost opened the door and stepped out into the hallway.

Frost saw Nifkawitz staring at him, then said, pointing back toward Marina's room, "Say a word about that and I'll slit your damn throat—and you know I don't make threats."

Nifkawitz nodded slightly, then said, "I got a meeting you gotta go to."

"What kind of meeting," and looking at his watch, he added, "at three A.M.?"

Nifkawitz glanced around the empty hall, then said, "State Department—down at the Embassy—now."

"Ughh," Frost groaned, then shrugging his shoulders said, "As the Bard of the home sales cosmetics company said, 'Lay on Nifkawitz.'"

Frost followed the man down the hallway and to the back stairs, nodded as he passed one of his own detail on duty by the rear entrance and walked out into the back driveway. There was a car there—some kind of medium-priced GM model a couple of years old. "Come on," Nifkawitz grunted.

"I can see why the government is so disorganized—three in the morning for a meeting. Jees—" Frost walked around in front of the car and got into the front passenger seat—but not before checking the rear seat for a reception committee. He still trusted none of the men who worked for him and now that he knew for sure Nifkawitz was one of the plants he trusted him even less. "Where we goin'?" Frost asked.

"The Embassy, I told ya'," Nifkawitz said testily.

"Oh, yeah, forgot—"

The streets in the "good" part of the city were deserted, save for the occasional troop transport. With the official Presidential plates on the car, the curfew didn't apply to them and no one stopped them.

The Embassy, walled with iron grillwork gates and iron grillwork ramparts to match above the walls, was at the far end of the local "embassy row" and one of the most impressive of the foreign ligations, visible a block farther down from the comparatively somber, massive Soviet Embassy they passed now.

"You goin' in the back way?" Frost asked.

"Yeah—nobody wants to advertise you just yet. You must be trusted—we weren't even followed from the Presidential Palace."

"You know why I'm trusted," Frost asked, then said, "because Aguillara-Garcia can trust me. And don't you jokers forget that," Frost grumbled.

They rounded the corner past the Embassy and turned into the side drive. There was a man waiting for them—a security guy by the look of him and the M-16 on his shoulder. The man waved them on after flashing a light into the front seat on

117

Frost's face. Frost smiled, "Get ye hence and fornicate with thyself," and they drove on.

"What, you lookin' for trouble?" Nifkawitz said as he turned the key off and started out of the car.

"Naw, not me," Frost answered, then followed Nifkawitz up the low flight of back steps and across the small stone porch and in through the service entrance. There was a long stairway ahead of them, Nifkawitz stepping aside to let Frost go ahead of him, Frost smiling and waiting until Nifkawitz moved up first. At the top of the stairs, he followed Nifkawitz around a corner into a long, narrow, paneled hallway. They stopped at the end of the hallway and Nifkawitz knocked on the oak-paneled Christian door.

"Come in," Frost heard, then followed Nifkawitz through the doorway into an office lit only by a bright desk lamp, flooding a green blotter in light and only revealing the lower half of the torso of the man sitting behind it.

"I'm Ambassadore Pilchner, Captain Frost, and you're going to say something funny like 'congratulations.'"

"I don't like voices when I can't see faces," Frost said to the man behind the desk, then felt in the darkness by the doorway and hit the light switch.

A large overhead chandelier illuminated and Frost squinted back at the man behind the desk. "I'd still say congratulations," Frost muttered, then walked toward the desk, deliberately standing at an oblique angle to it.

"What, do you think I have a gun mounted in the desk or something?" the Ambassadore asked.

"Let's put it this way—the reason I'm not sitting in that chair that's so neatly squared right across from you and the only one in the room besides yours isn't because I'm worried about sitting in it and getting a bayonet or a needle popping up and into my rectum—no, I'm not distrustful. Let's just be open with one another."

"You know, Captain Frost," the Ambassadore said, "even though you reside very little in the United States, you are an American citizen and as such, I work for you."

Frost smiled. "Fine, you're fired—spending too much on postage, stealing paperclips, I could go on but I won't."

The Ambassadore stood up. "Dammit man, there's a revolution going on outside these walls."

"And there wouldn't be," Frost said, leaning across the desk, his eye not more than a foot away from the Ambassadore's face, "if the U.S. Government had agreed to resupply Aguillara-Garcia. And he was even ready to pay for it. What's the matter, you guys only give military equipment to governments that want it for free?"

"I'm not here to argue politics with you, Captain Frost."

"You're not here? No—I'm the one who got outa bed at three A.M. for a meeting—why?"

Nifkawitz took a step closer to Frost, the muscles in his shoulders bunched, "What's a matter, miss that little hot piece—"

Frost didn't let him finish the sentence, started feigning a right by hauling his fist back, but smashed his left knee into Nifkawitz's crotch and

119

let him fall. Bending over the man, sprawled on the oriental rug, Frost said, "Remember that remark about an edged weapon and your throat a little while ago? Well, that's why I didn't let you finish your sentence—capische, fella?"

Nifkawitz nodded, groaning, and Frost stood up, then looked back toward the Ambassadore.

"You think you're pretty tough stuff, don't you, Frost? Well, I could snap my fingers right now and have you killed—you know that?"

Frost stared at the Ambassadore, then whispered, "So go snap."

The air seemed heavy between them, Frost thought, but he stood there, waiting for the Ambassadore to speak and after a moment, the Ambassadore sat back down and started talking.

"The situation here is deteriorating, dramatically. You know that. The reason you were hired by us is to do something no official U.S. representative could do—you are to come back here tomorrow morning with your mercenary force and lead us out of the country, over land to Mexico by truck and car. Ostensibly, you will be an American patriot, who views the situation here as deteriorating so badly that you are convinced the Embassy personnel are in danger of a takeover, as happened in Iran. Because of your private knowledge of the internal situation, we take your counsel and agree to leave, of course after consulting with Washington. This obviates the U.S. sending in troops to protect or evacuate us."

"What about the rest of the U.S. citizens here?"

"We doubt they are in real danger, and at the

120

moment their plight cannot be helped. We think that taking the Embassy staff out of the country will be sufficient to cool anti-American protest here and focus attention against the government—where I might add it justly belongs."

Frost lit a cigarette and stared past the Ambassadore for a moment, cooling his temper. "And what about my job protecting President Aguillara-Garcia."

"It is unfortunate, and we personally wish no harm to the President, but his fate is out of our hands, out of your hands too—you know that. He will now reap what the years of military dictatorship, the abridgement of civil rights, the abrogation of the voting process—what all of these have sown. I imagine he will be tried by the people and receive their justice."

Frost looked coldly at the Ambassadore, "Which means they'll break into the Presidential Palace and tear his body limb from limb."

"As the Portuguese say, 'Que sera, sera.'"

"Start singing and I'll punch you in the mouth," Frost grunted, then bending over and pulling Nifkawitz to his feet, Frost turned back to the Ambassadore and said, "Be ready to go by seven or seven-thirty—just pack weapons, food, water—burn all your documents or put 'em in the shredder. Bring plenty of medical supplies."

Nifkawitz following him, still partially doubled over, Frost walked to the doorway, turning when the Ambassadore called, "Oh, Captain Frost."

"Yes," Frost said, looking back across his shoulder.

"You are doing the sensible thing—for a moment there, I thought you might indulge in more heroics. You know, men like you, in your profession, can become hopelessly anachronistic. But I'm glad that in the final analysis you were able to come to grips with the enlightenment of modern political thinking. And please remember, your government will not let your fidelity go unrewarded."

Frost turned toward the door again, whistling low as he did.

"What's that you're whistling, Captain," the Ambassadore asked.

"Just a little ditty—you wouldn't recognize it," Frost said. But Nifkawitz did and looked at Frost—the "ditty" was the Star Spangled Banner.

Frost walked back along the hall and down the stairwell and stopped by the service entrance, waiting for Nifkawitz to catch up. Then Frost followed him back down the rear courtyard and back to the car. As Nifkawitz opened the driver's side door, Frost said, "You want me to drive?"

"Yeah," Nifkawitz groaned, "would ya'?"

Frost nodded, climbed in and reached across, popping open the passenger door. Nifkawitz slid in, bending awkwardly. As Frost gunned the small-sounding engine to life, Nifkawitz said, "Why the hell you clobber me like that back there, Frost?"

Frost made a U-turn in reverse, then drove across the courtyard and toward the rear gate, got the nod—an angry one—from the security man and turned out into the street, then rounded the corner back along Embassy Row.

"How many of them you got here—security men?" Frost asked.

"Just two—Ambassadore didn't want a big presence here."

Frost just nodded. "I'll answer your other question—why I popped you. See, my parents weren't around much when I was a kid—father in the Army, the whole routine, mother away, divorced. So I can't say I got it from my parents or anything, so maybe I'm just a natural chauvinist pig or something. I'll hit a woman if I have to, even shoot one. But what I do in bed with one isn't something I like other people talking about." Turning and flashing a grin toward Nifkawitz, Frost added, "Call me old fashioned, but I still believe a gentleman doesn't discuss his affairs with women."

"Man, you're crackers."

Frost didn't turn his head, just lit a cigarette and stared straight ahead, then talking through a cloud of smoke, said, "Call it what you will—just don't forget it." Gambling, Frost said, "How long you been a contract man?" If the guy was in CIA, Frost reasoned, he'd know what Frost meant and figure somehow Frost had found him out. If he wasn't, he'd think the reference was to working for the State Department.

"How'd you—"

"I didn't until you just told me," Frost remarked. "Now gimme the real scam—what's with that dum-dum Ambassadore and his Napoleon impression?"

123

"I can't tell you a thing man—at least nothing I wasn't supposed to tell you tomorrow morning."

"So tell me now," Frost said.

"Okay—once again the Company and State don't quite see eye-to-eye."

"I see eye-to-eye with everyone," Frost said, "but of course, I only have one eye."

"Hell man," Nifkawitz groaned. "Anyway, State wants Aguillara-Garcia thrown to the wolves, or at least it seems that way. The Company doesn't—he was loyal to us, still is. We want you to get him out, even if he doesn't want to come out."

"Anybody care what he wants, or I want? Don't even bother to answer that—when are you guys ever going to stop playing marbles with human beings? I'm crackers, huh? Well, you know what I'm going to do? I'm gonna get Aguillara-Garcia and his family out of the country because I want to do it, not because anyone else wants me to—and I'm popping off that jackass Ambassadore first time he tries to doublecross me. I came down here for a number for State and a number for Aguillara-Garcia, so I'm going to do both. I'm going to save the President's life whether he wants it or not, and I'll get the Embassy people out. Now you tell me one thing?"

"What?" Nifkawitz said, lighting a cigarette.

"Which of you guys are Company men and which of you guys are State men—since I don't trust any of you?"

"I don't know—I think there's one other Company man, at least that's what I was told, and my briefing officer told me too that there were

124

three State men. But I got no idea who's who."

As Frost pulled past the guard post at the Presidential Palace, he stopped the car a moment while the gates opened electronically. "I am not a bloodthirsty man, I hope everyone gets through this entire little diplomatic farce completely intact. However, I don't care what your orders are—just let me get my job done." Frost moved the car again, figuring his tough guy routine had about run its course. He was tired and the next time he'd get to grab some sleep was a long, long way off. He stopped the car behind the Palace, closing his eye a moment, tired. But with Nifka- witz still beside him, he kept the tips of his fingers close to the butt of his Browning pistol.

Chapter Ten

Frost stood alone in his room a moment. He'd showered and shaved in this place for the last time. If he ever did see the Presidential Palace again, he thought, it'd probably have a picture of Castro hanging out front and be some sort of People's Palace of Recreation. Frost was the fall guy; he knew that. Whatever happened right, the State Department would get the credit for it. If someone got killed—someone who mattered—he'd have the electric version of a short rope and a long drop waiting for him.

He sat on the edge of the bed, staring at himself across the room in the full-length mirror. Camouflage fatigues, combat boots—he didn't like jungle boots—a cammie slouch hat. Back right where he'd started, he thought. He stood up, slipped on the JerryRig diagonal shoulder holster, clipped the little Gerber MkI boot knife into his pants and caught up his back pack, swat bag and rifle.

Aguillara-Garcia would feel betrayed.

As Frost went through the door, not bothering to close it behind him, he decided that couldn't be helped. If betrayal was the only way to prevent Aguillara-Garcia from sacrificing his life for an unsalvageable cause, then betrayal it would be.

Frost walked down the hall and wound his way over to the guard room. All twelve of his mercenaries—all twelve of the men he didn't trust—were waiting for him. He stood in the doorway—not caring if anyone heard him from the hallway—and addressed them all. "You three, get outside the President's bedroom—don't let him out. From there, you can keep an eye on the First Lady—keep her in too."

Nifkawitz said, "Now don't get upset, but what about the girl?"

Frost looked at him and smiled. "She's waiting downstairs for me—I'll get her and bring her up to the President's suite. We get everyone dressed and over to the Embassy quick. You fix the telephone lines, Pearblossom?" Frost got a nod, then said,

"Anything I forgot?" Since there was no answer, he just nodded and picked up his rifle again and the pack and bag and headed downstairs, leaving everything but the rifle on the first landing. He walked around toward the back hall and entered the kitchen. When the old woman who was the cook saw him with the assault rifle in his hands she dropped the crockery milk pitcher she carried. Marina was waiting there for him, her eyes suddenly wide, staring at him. Frost turned back to the old woman. "Give me some coffee, mama, okay?"

She looked at him and nodded and Frost walked across the kitchen, stepping across the mess from the broken pitcher, leaning the CAR-16 into the corner nearest the empty chair at the little table across from Marina, then sat down.

"What is it, Hank—is my father sending you out into the jungle after the terrorists?"

"No, honey," Frost said, lighting a cigarette.

"Then why are you dressed like that; why do you have your rifle?"

"I'm pulling the plug." He looked at her, then realized the Americanism was something she didn't understand. "I'm getting you, your step-mother and your father out of the country, along with the staff of the U.S. Embassy."

"Pero, no—But no, Hank. My father will not leave here; you know that."

"Yes," Frost murmured, then looking down into the coffee the cook had placed on the table in front of him, taking the pitcher for the last time and pouring milk into the big coffee mug the old woman kept for him, he said, "I know he won't want to go voluntarily—he'll probably always hate me, if we live through this. But I can't leave him here to die. He's your father," Frost said, his voice somehow sounding awkward, the words hard to form, "but let's just say I feel for him too. I'm not leaving him here to be a dead martyr— period. And I don't want any trouble from you."

Marina started to get up. Frost looked up at her, saying, "Don't make me deck you, kid. But don't leave my sight either."

She stood there a moment, then put her hands behind her, smoothing her skirt under her as she sat down. "Where are you taking us?" she said.

"To Mexico—guy from the U.S. Embassy has his own escape route all planned out—figure we may as well take advantage of it, at least for a while."

"What if my father doesn't want to go, Hank?"

"I'll make him."

"How will you make him?"

"I'll take my pistol and put it to Anna's head if I have to, and you and I both know that if I really did have to, I'd pull the trigger. She's the one member of your family I consider expendable—bear that in mind."

Frost finished his coffee and walked with Marina across the kitchen, stopping to give the old woman cook an affectionate kiss on the cheek and get a chuckle from her when he whispered in her ear, "Esta muy bonita, mama." He reached for

Marina's hand then and, hesitantly at first, she took it, walking with him through the back hallway and up to the landing where he snatched up his pack, then up the stairs to the second floor. Her fingers stiffened in his when she saw the mercenary guards in front of her father's door, Frost whispering to her, "Relax, if he ran out there in the street, he'd be killed."

Frost knocked on the oaken double doors and heard no response from inside. He tried the knob and the door wasn't locked, so he let Marina walk in first, shouting, "Sir, your daughter is going in ahead of me—don't shoot."

Frost followed through the doorway, inside. Closing the doors behind him and placing his packs and his rifle by the door, he spotted Aguillara-Garcia, fully dressed, sitting in a brocaded chair by the sheer curtains covering the windows, the sun just starting to fade their whiteness into pink.

Marina said nothing, neither did her father. "El Presidente," Frost said. "I wish to speak with you."

"Why are you doing this, Capitan Frost?" Aguillara-Garcia still didn't move.

"Look, sir, I know you've got that revolver, I know you can kill me. And you know exactly why I'm here. To do the same thing I've been doing these last weeks—save your life. Only this time whether you want me to or not."

"Don't you see, amigo," the President said, turning toward him at last. "You do not under-

130

stand. Monte Azul is my home. You cannot ask me to leave it. I would rather die here than run, than live somewhere else."

Frost crossed the room toward the President's chair, feeling awkward walking across the delicate oriental rug there with his combat boots. Stopping a few feet from the President, close enough to see the revolver in his hand, Frost said, "Sir, I happen to feel that keeping you alive is more important than fighting a battle you cannot win against the terrorists, the students—even your friends. You can trust virtually no one—" Frost felt uncomfortable and conspicuous saying that. "And you are running out of ammunition, replacement parts for your equipment—everything. At least for the time being, a Communist takeover here is inevitable. If you die, you're doing just what they want. But if you live, you can go on fighting the Communists and help to save other countries from falling to them, perhaps someday return." Frost knew that last was a lie and wasn't vain enough to entertain the hope that Aguillara-Garcia saw it any differently either.

"If I do not choose to go, how will you make me?" the President said.

Frost sighed heavily. "If I cannot physically subdue you, I will threaten and take if necessary the life of your wife—I mean that."

Aguillara-Garcia considered that a moment, then looked down at his pistol and raised it slowly, the engraved Python like a bizarre mechanical jewel there in his hand. "And if I kill you with this?"

Frost lied, "I've given orders for your wife to be executed—and besides, sir, although I'm sure you cannot see it now, I think you've had your fill of shooting friends with that, haven't you?"

Frost took a few steps forward, holding out his hand for the gun. The President did not move. But after a moment, he took the pistol, turned it over in his hand and held it out. Frost took the gun, looked at it a moment, then turned the pistol butt forward in his hand. "You might need this, Presidente."

"As of now," Aguillara-Garcia said, his voice lifeless sounding, "that title has become meaningless."

Flatly, slowly, deliberately, Frost said, "No sir, it hasn't—El Presidente. Perhaps Marina," Frost added, "can help you to pack for several days of hard travel, and please bring as much ammunition for that revolver as you can carry—" Frost didn't finish the rest of his sentence. It would have been superfluous, he thought.

Under a very "loose" guard, Aguillara-Garcia and Marina came down the staircase into the main hall for the last time, an elegant-looking briefcase under the President's arm. Stopping by several large packing cases in the hallway, three of Frost's men loading them out the back door, Aguillara-Garcia said, "And what is this, Capitan Frost? I would not have expected you to plunder."

Frost said nothing, Marina bending to look inside the open top of one of the boxes. He heard her say to her father, "These are the things from your office, father, Hank is saving them for you."

"They will serve to remind me of here—and heighten my bitterness."

Frost watched silently as Pearblossom ushered the President and his daughter to a waiting jeep, the top up less for protection from the elements than to disguise the passengers it would carry.

And then Anna walked down the staircase. She came over to Frost. "I know you mean well, Capitan Frost—and I know you would not have me killed."

Frost had no idea how she had found out about what he had said, and before he could answer her, she had already walked past him out to the waiting jeep.

Frost hitched up the pack over his left arm, the SWAT bag in his left hand, his right hand on his rifle. He shot a glance to Nifkawitz—"That everything?"

"Sure is, Captain."

Cocking his head toward the back door, Frost said, "Then let's go."

The drive to Embassy Row was quiet—with the Army vehicles and the official look of the caravan, they were not stopped by the soldiers enforcing the martial law throughout the city. As they passed Commacho's headquarters, in the lead jeep, the vehicle just ahead of the President, Frost thought that he needn't worry about never seeing the portly General again. He knew full well Commacho would be after him within hours, blood in his eye, murder in his heart. And Frost respected Commacho for it. Ironically, he thought, Commacho would do anything he could to save Aguillara-Garcia's life, just as Frost was doing—anything short of going against his President and friend's wishes.

Frost leaned back, closing his eye, grumbling to Pearblossom who was driving him, "Once around the park and take it nice and easy on the curves, pal."

They reached the American Embassy without incident, unable to take so many vehicles into the courtyard behind it, so they parked alongside the rear Embassy wall.

Only Frost's jeep and the jeep carrying Aguillara-Garcia and his family entered. There were no security men in view, but guarding the front and rear exit he could see six fatigue-clad Marines each, M-16s at the ready, Smith & Wesson .38 Special revolvers on their hips rather than .45 autos—the wisdom of the lighter revolver round for Embassy guards always eluded Frost.

They were expecting him, apparently, and Frost walked past them, leaving Pearblossom to watch the jeep with the First Family, taking Nifkawitz inside with him. In the hallway, the Ambassadore was waiting, a pudgy woman whom Frost hoped wasn't the guy's wife beside him. "Ahh, Captain Frost," he said. Seeing Frost looking at the woman, he added, "This is my secretary, Miss Cardon."

Frost smiled, "Hi!" Then turning to the

Ambassadore, he said, "You ready, all the Embassy personnel ready to go? All the weapons and ammo loaded up, files burned, the whole routine?"

"Relax, Captain Frost," the Ambassadore said. "We're all ready to go. Does President Aguillara-Garcia know you've gone?"

"Oh, yeah," Frost said. "Couldn't avoid it."

"Hmm, I hope that doesn't prove unfortunate. You don't think he'll try to stop us."

"No," Frost said, "I know he won't."

As they walked toward the rear exit, the Ambassadore, seeming to have thought a moment and considered Frost's answer, said, "How can you be so sure, Captain, that Aguillara-Garcia won't attempt to stop us? I know you two got along well, but—"

"Oh, I'm sure all right, Mr. Ambassadore—Aguillara-Garcia is sitting right outside in a jeep—he's coming along with us."

They were halfway down the stairs leading out the back entrance. The Ambassadore stopped, stared at Frost then took a step down and looked out into the courtyard and the two jeeps waiting there, one with the top up. "You're joking, Captain!"

"Me—you know I never joke, Mr. Ambassadore," Frost said, smiling. He walked down the rest of the steps and toward his own jeep. Behind him he could hear the Ambassadore saying, "Nifkawitz—do something."

Frost turned around, saying, "Mr. Ambassadore. You can haul out all your Marine guard, the security guys, maybe all of them can stop me. But not before I put a bullet in your head." Frost swung up the muzzle of the CAR-16 and pointed it toward the Ambassadore's face. "Now no one's forcing you to come along—you can just stay here and we'll go without you—but after I essentially kidnapped the President of this country, I doubt American officials would be too popular around here. Your choice—I'm leaving in—" and Frost glanced down to this watch—"three minutes." He took a few steps back, felt the jeep's right front fender behind him with his left hand and backed toward the front passenger seat, then put one leg inside and sat on the edge of the seat, all the time his CAR-16's muzzle never once wavering from the Ambassadore's head.

Ambassadore Pilchner stood there a moment, unmoving, then once again apparently reaching a decision, shouted across the courtyard to Frost, "You leave me very little choice, Captain Frost. But let me assure you that your conduct will be reported to the highest authorities."

Frost looked back, laughing, and said, "Don't scare me that way."

It took quite a bit more than three minutes to get the secretaries, the Marines and the other two dozen or so members of the Embassy staff loaded aboard the trucks and jeeps, since most of the vehicles, driven by his own mercenaries, were ones Frost was providing courtesy of the Presidential Palace motorpool and the Army of the Republic of

Monte Azul.

As they finally got started, backtracking for a distance along Embassy Row toward the main boulevard which would lead them onto the highway past the airport and then onto the narrow roads across the closest portion of the jungle, Frost once again told Pearblossom to take it easy—he wanted to sleep. Closing his right eye, knowing at the back of his mind he could not sleep despite his tiredness, he found himself assessing his situation. General Commacho would be after him to rescue the President. The terrorists would be after him soon also, to kill the President and try to take the U.S. Embassy staff hostage. There was more or less a half thousand miles to cross—virtually all jungle with some mountains—until they reached the border with Mexico. There was the matter of his own men, too. So far, Nifkawitz was the only one he had pegged, a CIA man working undercover in State Department Intelligence. But was Nifkawitz telling him all the truth, Frost wondered? He doubted that was possible—perhaps Nifkawitz didn't even know the truth. The other eleven mercenaries, even Pearblossom, who was driving him, were still unknown quantities, and because of that Frost could not trust them. At least one other was a CIA man, that man perhaps posing as one of the other State Department people, but Frost couldn't be sure of that.

At least, Frost thought, smiling to himself, it was a perfectly even-handed situation. He could trust absolutely no one—even the girl Marina, though they were lovers, would probably stab him in the back if she thought she were helping her father. He forced himself to try and get some sleep, because once night came, with no one to trust, even the woman he might be sharing a bed of sorts with, sleep could well be terminal.

Chapter Eleven

"Hey, Captain, you ain't sleepin'."

It was Pearblossom's voice, and Pearblossom was right, Frost thought—he wasn't sleeping. "Yeah, what is it, Herb?"

As Frost opened his eye and looked around him, he saw they were nearing the airport—just as well Pearblossom had kept him from falling asleep. If there was going to be an attack by the student militants or the terrorists before they got away from the city, this was the logical area—when the caravan would have to slow down in the open to turn off the dead-ending highway and onto the jungle road.

"Hey, Captain—you were gonna tell us back there in Miami before we came down here—how you got that eyepatch?"

Out of reflex action, Frost said, "Well, it's not much of a story, really . . ." Then, Frost's gray-green right eye lighting up, the smile frown lines in his cheeks creasing, he said, "Back in the days when I was going to college, this one summer I came down to Florida and got a summer job working in one of those marine amusement parks—you know, the big aquariums, the performing killer whales, the seals, the whole routine. Well, I'd always been interested in languages—was an English major in college. Anyway, I was fascinated with dolphins. You know, Herb, they're mammals, just like we are, and a great deal of intensive research has been conducted to attempt to communicate with them. Imagine, if you will," Frost went on, "that some day man could have a partner on this earth, a nonhuman partner of essentially equal intelligence whose abilities would allow him to explore the very depths of the vast oceans of the world, to farm the sea with previously unheard of agricultural methods. It's thrilling," Frost said, lighting a Camel. "Well, you can imagine how excited I was after a time when the dolphin trainer, knowing my interest in these cunningly intelligent little creatures, invited me to help him work with them."

140

"You pullin' my leg, man?"

"Who? Me?" Frost asked, incredulously.

Then, going on, Frost said, "Well, at any event, working with the dolphins was such a unique experience. And, let me tell you, those little guys are smart. After just a few days, even I—a novice, mind you, at dolphin training—was already teaching them tricks. I remember one dolphin—I could never forget him," Frost said, tugging at his eyepatch. "His name was Irving—Irving the Dolphin we used to call him. Catchy, isn't it?" Frost asked.

Then, without waiting for Pearblossom to answer, "Well, this one afternoon the orphanage nearby was getting a special performance. They only took in kids who were one-quarter black, one-quarter Oriental and half Swedish. Beautiful little kids—epicanthic eyelids, blond curly hair—I tell ya'. But, anyway, we had this special performance going on. Irving and I were trying a new trick. Wanted to teach those little boys and girls the evils of cigarette smoking—show them that their pal Irving the Dolphin knew that smoking was bad for your health. Well, this was the first time Irving and I had ever tried the trick in public. I held this cigarette in my mouth—wasn't lit because we didn't want Irving to burn himself or anything. I'd lean over the edge of the diving platform and Irving would leap up when the head trainer rang this little bell. Then he'd snatch the cigarette.

"Well," Frost went on, "as I said, Irving and I were both a little nervous. He jumped out of the

141

water—so gracefully—and as he did, I accidentally leaned a little too far forward—just my desire to do well, I guess. Anyway, Irving missed the cigarette—and you know those narrow blunt little noses the dolphins have . . . You can guess the rest. The trainer even had Irving retrieve my eye from the bottom of the Dolphin pool, in the vain hope the wonderful surgeons at Day-Nite Drive-In Memorial Industrial Hospital nearby would be able somehow to put it back. Irving—poor little dolphin—thought it was a fish snack, though, and ate it.''

Frost turned and looked away out the window. Behind him, he heard Pearblossom saying, ''Aw, come on, man—you're kiddin', right?''

Frost turned around, sniffed loudly and brushed his right index finger at his good eye, as though to hold back a tear. ''Would I jest about something like that?''

As Pearblossom started to answer him, Frost heard or felt something odd. He turned back and stared out the window. Without looking away, he snapped to Pearblossom, ''We got company over on the right behind the far side of the airport fence—I can't tell how many yet.''

''What are we gonna do?''

''More importantly, who are they?'' Frost said, lighting another cigarette. Then, ''Okay—we're sittin' ducks on this highway, and if they haven't opened up yet that means the killing ground's up the road. Pull off to the side and give a hand signal to get all the other vehicles to do the same. Put this whole road between us, cross the median strip into

142

the lanes going into the city."

Pearblossom, his left arm stretched outside the jeep as though for a turn signal, the arm waving frantically, wrenched the steering wheel to the left, cutting across the deserted two lanes of blacktop, onto the sandy median strip and into the opposing lanes. Already, Frost could see the first puff from a mortar along the opposite side of the road. As Pearblossom started slowing the jeep having reached the opposite shoulder, he said to Frost, "How'd they know it was us, Captain?"

"They didn't," Frost said, "probably still don't know who we got in the jeeps—probably some terrorists just waiting along the road for whoever comes by—just happened to be us. If they can mess up troop movements into the city—they were positioned for that—then they can help the student rioters." As the jeep ground to a halt, gravel crunching under the wheels, Frost started out the doorless passenger side and shouted to Pearblossom, "Come on, man!"

The CAR-16 in his hands, its selector on full auto, Frost started across the median strip, shouting to Pearblossom, "Leave Nifkawitz in charge, you come with any five of the others and try to bring a couple of the Embassy Marines!" Alone, Frost crossed the roadway, long-distance heavy machinegun fire raining down on him, the puff of the mortar from behind the fence as incessant as a bothersome, deadly, insect. Without bothering to aim—at two hundred yards the distance was too great for casual marksmanship—Frost loosed several three-round bursts at the terrorist position.

Diving toward a pothole beside the airport fence as at last he made it across the road—the mortar rounds were hitting close in now, its operator knowing what he was doing and walking it on target—Frost hauled himself up by the fence in a low crouch, moving the selector on the CAR-16 to semi auto and firing aimed single shots along the side of the fence. He wished silently for a scope.

Across the road, Frost could see Pearblossom, six of the mercenaries with him, three of the Marines, and two three-piece suit types from the Embassy security detail. Pearblossom in their lead, the twelve men broke into a dead run across the median strip. Frost levered up to full auto fire again and started hammering bursts of three rounds each along the fence, the reinforcements firing their weapons full auto as they dodged and ran. "Zigged when he should of zagged," Frost thought as one of the security men doubled up, half vaulting into mid air, then hit the tarmac road surface like a stone against water. The CAR-16 in his right hand, Frost fired as he left the cover of the fence and ran into the road, past Pearblossom and the others and grabbed the security man by the collar of his coat, then dragged him toward the comparative shelter of the fence.

Comparative was the word, Frost thought, the mortar rounds homing in closer with each firing.

"Gotta knock out that mortar," Frost rasped to Pearblossom and the others as he crouched in their midst, the young security man—badly wounded

144

and unconscious—beside him. "Take care of him," Frost said, pointing to one of his Mercs. "Pearblossom, take five men as maneuver element, cross the fence and cut diagonally to the far side of the other fence, then cross over. I'm taking four men and moving up along this fence line for a frontal." Looking to Pearblossom, he rasped, "Got me?"

"Right, Captain."

Frost took the three remaining Marines and Kilner, one of his Mercs, and started up along the wall, swapping to a fresh magazine in the CAR-16 as he moved out.

"Let's go," he rasped, "run it out." There was nothing for it but a straight frontal assault with the weapons and manpower they had available, and Frost wanted it over with. In a dead run single file, Frost and his men charged forward along the fence, moving too fast for the mortar to be of any effect. The machinegun fire was heavy, one of his Mercs, Kilner, going down with a hit in the leg. They left him there, but still firing along the fence wall to support them. As they reached the midway point—Frost could see Pearblossom and his men nearly to the corner of the far fence—friendly fire from the Mercs and half dozen marines across the road opened up against the enemy position. Nifkawitz had disobeyed orders and used his initiative, Frost thought, grateful for it. Nifkawitz was using the residual force across the road as a second maneuver element. Less than fifty yards from the enemy position, breathless from the run and the fear, Frost and the others dropped to the ground, forming a small wedge and laying down heavy automatic weapons fire on the terrorist position. Once Pearblossom had crossed the far fence wall, Frost signaled to the Marines behind him and they took up the running assault again, the fire from Pearblossom's men and the men under Nifkawitz from across the road intensifying and catching the terrorists in a crossfire.

It seemed like only seconds to Frost and then they had closed with the enemy—a dozen and a half well-armed terrorists. The range between opposing forces less than a dozen yards, the firing was point-blank, the smell of burning flesh and the sound of gunfire everywhere.

Out of ammo, Frost tried changing sticks on the CAR-16. A terrorist with an AK-47, bayonet fixed below the muzzle, stormed toward him. Dropping to his left side, Frost used a scissor kick and caught the man at the ankles, then jumped toward him, the spearpoint boot knife in Frost's left fist, his right knee smashing hard into the terrorist's groin, then the knife biting deep into the man's neck.

On his feet again, Frost had the AK-47 in his hands, firing it into the wall of terrorists until it was empty, then going in with the bayonet and taking out two more men before he turned, the rifle in a guard position, the edge of the bayonet tipped red with blood as he spun on his heels and suddenly stopped.

Frost remembered then to breathe, happy he still could. All eighteen terrorists were dead—a quick scan of the ground and the way the bodies lay told him that. Kilner had crawled up after them, or somehow made it with the wounded leg. One of the Marines who'd come with Frost was clamping his left shoulder tight in his right hand, the hand covered with blood, a worn-blue .38 Special revolver in his left hand, a terrorist dead at his feet with his face shot away.

Pearblossom was limping. When he apparently spotted Frost looking at him, he said, "Twisted my ankle comin' over that fence back there—I'm okay."

Frost nodded. Dropping the AK-47 to the ground beside him, he walked back and retrieved his knife from the throat of the terrorist he'd killed with it. He found his CAR-16 under the body of another terrorist, checked that it was functional and loaded a fresh magazine into the well, then snapped back the bolt, putting the safety on.

Lighting a cigarette, Frost looked across the road at Nifkawitz, shouted, "Any casualties?" and Nifkawitz signaled a negative, then Frost yelled again, "Get those Marines over here with the doctor from the Embassy staff—got some casualties here."

Frost turned to Pearblossom, saying, "You got it man," then walked slowly across the road. There was a civilian truck coming and Frost dropped to one knee in the road, telescoping the stock out on the CAR-16 and flipping the selector to full auto. But the truck stopped and two men, perhaps in their sixties, climbed out with their hands in the air.

Frost got to his feet. Even from twenty yards away, the one-eyed man could see the truck was filled with stalks of green bananas.

Chapter Twelve

"Just where the hell have you taken us, Captain Frost? I demand to know!"

Frost tossed his camouflage crusher hat back onto the seat of the jeep and pulled a Camel from the pack in the breast pocket of his fatigue blouse, lighting it with the battered Zippo he always used. "Look, Mr. Ambassadore—this is a railroad, see? Tracks, engine, cars—the whole thing. You've seen trains before."

"God damn you, sir! Why are we here?"

Frost turned his back to the Ambassadore—it was either that or hit him in the face, Frost figured. Then turning again to face the man, he said, "Look, pal—there is one road through the jungle—the terrorists 'll be all over it like a $39.95 carpet sale from the Late Show on TV. I can't walk it out of here; we've got wounded, we've got older women—like your secretary—and we've got just too damned much junk, food, water, documents, weapons. You know. This railroad line leads straight into Mexico, it runs through the jungle and the mountains and there should be wood all along the way that we can burn. Just think of it this way—if you went to an amusement park you'd probably pay as much as $2.50 just to ride a train that looked like this! I'm givin' it to ya for free."

Pilchner said nothing more, but stomped back toward his jeep. Frost just looked at him as he walked away, smiling. Pearblossom, by Frost's right shoulder, said, "Why don't you just smoke that sucker?"

Frost said, "Gee—I wish I'd thought of that! Here, wait a minute. I'll call him back," then throwing his hands up in disgust Frost walked away, toward the engine.

The rail yard was deserted, abandoned. But the engine, aside from a profusion of vines entwined over parts of it, appeared intact. He'd checked the place out with a helicopter pilot taking him there two weeks earlier—the engine still had all its controls and there were no holes in the boiler. As best as the pilot—also a damned good mechanic,

Frost had thought—could detect, the engine should still be serviceable. Silently now, Frost prayed the man had been right.

"Pearblossom," he shouted.

"Yes, Captain."

"Get up a detail to get this thing running, fired up, the works. Then clean out the three best and most accessible of the railroad cars—we'll need 'em. Then once we've got this thing rollin' we'll get everything aboard. Got me?"

"Yeah, Captain," the man shouted back, then turned and started rousting the manpower for the job.

Catching a few minutes sleep when he could, as did the men under him and the people from the Embassy staff, Frost labored through the night. No one there had ever stoked a wood-burning furnace before and though the engine itself did prove of "one piece" and operational, cutting the wood, stabilizing the steam pressure—all the details that frontier railroad men of a century earlier had taken as matter of course—had to be tended to by men who discovered them as they went along. Several times during the long night, the flies thick around the lights they worked near, exhaustion leading to small accidents that produced cuts, abrasions, even a broken finger on one of the Embassy men, Frost remarked in all seriousness that he wished someone had left them an instruction booklet. But there was none and, through trial and error, by morning the locomotive—a small brass plate showed it had been built

151

in 1887—was operational and the spur leading to the switch track had been cleared and repaired.

A coal car was already coupled to the engine, this now filled to overflowing with wood from the nearby rain forest. After careful yet nonetheless hair-raising practice runs, Pearblossom was able to back the locomotive slowly enough to get into position for a manual coupling with the first of the three coach cars—there was no caboose. By eleven in the morning, far later than Frost liked, the train was assembled and everyone was aboard. Then the arduous three-mile trek beside the train began for Frost and his men along the spur route up to the main track, improvising repairs every foot of the way. The sought-for switch was frozen from decades of disuse and freeing that took almost an hour. Marina and Miss Cardon, the Ambassadore's secretary, and some of the other women from the Embassy staff got up a hearty lunch and continued keeping the coffee coming as they had in weary shifts all through the night. By fifteen minutes past noon, the train was on the main track, all passengers were aboard again and Frost had set his men and some of the marines on the roofs of the passenger cars as guards.

"Go ahead," Frost said. "Say it, Pearblossom."

Standing behind the controls of the engine, his shirt gone, his arms rippling with muscles under a thin veneer of sweat and dirt, Pearblossom grinned back at Frost, turned his head through the aperture and looked back along the train, then pulling on the rope for the steam whistle, shouted, "All aboard!" He jerked the whistle three times and let out the throttle. Almost painfully, the engine started to grind forward, the wheels slipping on the track a moment, then catching and the train moving out.

Leaning back on the fireman's stool, Frost lit a Camel and said, "Hot damn—you got her going Pearblossom."

Pearblossom, still grinning ear to ear, said, "Yeah—don't I though!"

Finishing the cigarette and almost superfluously tossing more wood into the boiler, Frost climbed up over the edge of the coal car and clambered across it then down, jumping onto the cast-iron railed platform of the lead passenger car, wrenching the door open and stepping inside. Aguillara-Garcia was sitting in the back of the car, just staring out the half-open window. As Frost started to move through the car, Anna, the First Lady, came toward him. "Hank," she whispered. "Tonight we can be alone again—I can make arrangements for us to be together in the center car. Oh, I want your body Hank—my Capitan."

Using the fatigue blouse to wipe the sweat from his chest and arms, Frost put the shirt over his left shoulder and stared at her. "Go—to—hell," he said very deliberately.

"What is this?"

"This is a refusal, lady, a put-down, a turn-off— a big fat NO. Claro, senora?"

"I wouldn't say that, Hank," she said, her voice low, almost menacing.

"I just did, lady."

"I will tell my husband how you seduced me, forced me to sleep with you—he will kill you."

Frost looked at her. "He doesn't have a firing squad to put me in front of anymore—maybe it's time he knew the truth about you anyway."

"Aguillara-Garcia will believe me. Phillipe will want to rip your other eye out with his bare hands, to shoot you—he will see you dead!"

"He may see us all dead, doesn't that dawn on you? Don't you have anything less petty than my not jumping in bed with you to worry about? I'm trying to save your husband's life, your stepdaughter's life—your life."

"What kind of life is that?" Anna said, looking away from him a moment. "A life in the public eye—siempre. I am supposed to be the ideal wife—dressed beautifully, socially active, concerned, saying nothing—I do not want this life!"

"What am I going to say?" Frost asked rhetorically, for a moment feeling almost genuine sympathy for her. "You made your life, you've been trying all these years with guys like me in order to escape it, and now there isn't any escape left. I'm sorry."

"I will tell my husband. He will kill you!"

"And what, Anna, will that prove—that men will die for you? I'll tell you something. A man doesn't die for a woman because she can squeeze her rear end into a tight dress or because she wants to hop into bed with him—that's all well and good. Your husband would die for you and I wouldn't—that's because he loves you and I don't. That's the difference—don't waste that." Lighting a cigarette, snatching up the CAR-16 he'd leaned into the corner by the door, Frost walked down the aisle of the car. He passed Aguillara-Garcia who apparently didn't notice him, then Frost crossed over into the next car. This center car was largely empty now except for a few of the Embassy people and one of Frost's Mercs. There were a large number of crates of supplies and ammunition. Frost sat down in an empty seat, his left elbow resting on a case of .38 Special ammo brought for the revolvers the Marines carried.

Stubbing out his cigarette on the floor, he looked up as the door behind him opened. As he'd almost expected, it was President Aguillara-Garcia, Anna standing beside him, clinging to his left arm. Even with the coat of his military uniform open and somewhat dirty, Aguillara-Garcia, for all his years, made an impressive figure.

"Capitan Frost—my wife—she has told me of what you did to her."

Frost stood up and turned to face the President, leaning back and away from him rather than standing close—not wanting to try to look menacing. "I did nothing to her, sir, nothing she didn't ask me to do, nothing she didn't threaten that I do or she would get you to have me shot."

"Liar!" Aguillara-Garcia almost spat out the words, slapping Frost across the face with his left hand. Frost didn't move. Aguillara-Garcia slapped him again, using his right hand this time. When Frost still did not respond, the older man began slapping Frost, again and again. The left corner of Frost's mouth was trickling blood.

The President's face almost purple with rage, Aguillara-Garcia took a step back, steadying himself with his hand against the seat back. "You are not a man of honor, Capitan!"

Frost looked at him hard and at Anna even harder. "I won't hit you, if that's what you mean—your wife has hurt you more than I ever could."

At that, Aguillara-Garcia, his rage seemingly out of control, threw his hands to Frost's throat and, to keep from being choked, Frost pushed him away. The President slumped back against the seat, then started toward him again, his eyes almost bulging from his sockets, his left hand going to his throat. He fell back. Frost bent toward him, catching Aguillara-Garcia in his arms before he hit the floor, then easing him into the seat he himself had occupied moments earlier.

Marina was beside him. "I saw all of it."

"There's no time for that now—get the Embassy doctor and watch him like a hawk—I don't know whose side he'd be on." Then turning and looking up at Anna standing there in the doorway, her right hand in the pocket of her dress, the fingertips of her left hand over her mouth—shock in her eyes—he said to her, "If President Aguillara-Garcia dies, you'll be the one who murdered him." She took a step back, staring now at Frost's face. Frost said, standing up and resting the President's head on the seat back, "And if he dies, bitch, I'm gonna rip your heart out with my bare hands and grind it into the floor. That's if you've got a heart."

Chapter Thirteen

Frost and Pearblossom were the only two of the fifty or so persons aboard the train who could run the engine, and Frost largely by dint of watching Pearblossom, Pearblossom largely by dint of a strong "sixth sense" where things mechanical were concerned. Frost sat, now alone in the engine cab, boring through the night. They were still cutting through the rain forest and because of the danger of deadfall trees their "speeding" was a scant thirty miles per hour, but with the beam of the aircraft landing light Pearblossom had rigged to the front of the engine, run off liberated storage batteries in the cab taken from the jeeps they had left behind, at least he could see something. The coal car behind the engine was nearly empty of wood and in the morning, at first light, Frost planned a refueling stop. By this same time the following night, Frost judged, they should be into or very near Mexico—if the engine and the little used track held out.

Hearing a noise behind him, he turned, the Browning High Power ripped out of the JerryRig shoulder holster he wore across his bare back. "Marina? How the hell—"

"I put on a pair of slacks, put the food I wanted to bring you in an old sack and did just like you and Pearblossom do to get up here—I climbed across the wood in the coal car."

There was a flashlight in her hand—he recognized it as his, the Safariland Kel-Lite he'd had stashed in the black rip-stop nylon SWAT bag. She looked down at the light in her hand, saying, "It was good that I borrowed this—I searched your pack and your bag until I found it. The level of wood inside the coal car is low."

"Yeah," Frost groaned, turning back to look up the track. "We'll stop to pick up more wood at daybreak. How's your father?" he asked, changing the subject.

"The doctor from the Embassy is with him—you needn't worry about the doctor. He seems to be a good man. My father is resting comfortably—it was not a major heart attack, gracias a Dios."

"Amen to that," Frost added.

"I saw the whole thing, this afternoon. You must love my father very much," she said quietly.

The word shocked him a bit—had he ever loved a man, Frost wondered? You were supposed to love your father—he had rarely seen him, and the few close friends he'd ever had were dead. Frost said nothing, but heard her behind him, then turned and watched her digging through the sack she had brought, bringing out a large thermos and pouring coffee for him. "How can you tell in the dark when the coffee cup is full?" she asked.

"You can't without burning your fingers," Frost answered. "Stick one of your fingers about a half inch below the rim of the cup on the inside and stop when you feel the coffee touch your finger—blind people do it that way, sort of Braille coffee pouring."

"Do you know a lot about blind people, Hank?"

"What, because of the eye?" he asked. Then, "I've looked into it a bit—no pun intended for a change. Taught myself the alphabet in Braille a long time ago—after I lost my eye I was seized with a kind of paranoia, I guess. You lose one eye you can't help but worry about losing the other one someday."

"Do you ever tell anyone the truth about it?"

"No."

"You are a good man—I was angry with you yesterday morning for forcing my father to do something he was opposed to. But I understand now why you did it. You genuinely wanted to do what you thought was best to save his life—and I

160

think you were right."

"Don't tell your father that," Frost said. "He's got enough people he thinks have turned against him—you're the only one left he can trust."

Beside him now, he felt her reach up and touch her lips to his cheek. "He should know," she said as she handed Frost the coffee cup, "about Anna, about why you are doing this—everything."

"When he's better then," Frost said, trying to get off the subject.

"What if he recovers enough to shoot you before then?" she asked, taking the cup from his free hand and handing Frost a sandwich. "This is the last of the fresh meat—eat it."

He glanced toward her. "Your father won't shoot me, and if he tries, I'll take my chances."

"What, you will stand there and let him kill you?"

Frost had no answer for her and didn't try to manufacture one. "Good sandwich, Marina," he said through a mouthful of bread and meat.

"Gracias," she said absently, then, "what is really going on—you seem to be caught in the middle of something and fighting your way out of it."

Nodding, despite the fact that she probably couldn't see his face well in the darkness, he said, "Aptly put, my dear—aptly put indeed. You want to know what's going on? Fine. Pull up the fireman's chair—after you toss a few pieces of wood in the boiler—I'll tell you all about it."

Two minutes later Frost was recounting the whole story—desperately needing an ally, more psychological than physical now. He told her everything, from his encounter on the ski slopes with her uncle's assassins to the blackmail he'd submitted to in order to get out of the Swiss jail, the State Department ploy to get him down to Monte Azul and at the same time set up her father.

"Your government would not do such a terrible thing," she said at last.

"Oh, you're right, kid—my government wouldn't, not even my State Department, but some of the men in it would. Why is beyond me. But nobody has bothered to tell me why anyway."

"Do you think the terrorists are following us? Or General Commacho?"

Frost, the last of the sandwich still in his mouth, lit a cigarette, the flame of the Zippo lighter like a torch against the darkness of the rain forest through which they traveled. After a moment Frost said, "I think it's a toss-up who finds us first—Commacho or the terrorists. For your sake, I hope it's Commacho. I'm dead anyway you look at it. So, I guess I hope nobody finds us. Once we get to Mexico I've got problems enough waiting for me with Ambassadore Pilchner. Your father is tight with the Mexican Government so he'll probably try to have me arrested. Yeah," Frost said, snapping his cigarette into the mouth of the boiler past the open cast iron door, "I've really set myself up just great this time. Made some good moves, I tell ya."

"You made one move that was very good," Marina whispered, her lips touching his ear. "You took me to your bed—has that been good for you?"

"I'm not gonna win any medals for that either though, once your father finds out, kid."

Frost could barely make out her face in the sparse light from the open boiler of the locomotive. "Then if we are doomed as lovers, let us seal it," she whispered.

He looked at her, saying, "Where'd you read that? You're not a romance novel addict, are you?"

"Be serious, Hank," she said, and taking her at her word, Frost hooked his right arm around her and drew her close to him, kissing her lips, a taste of salt on them—she was crying.

"What's the matter, kid?" he asked.

She didn't answer him, although he could hear her start to several times, but after a few moments she just rested her head on his shoulder there in the darkness, the light Frost watched up along the track burning a yellow-white hole in the velvet blackness ahead.

Pearblossom had relieved Frost at two A.M. and Frost had taken Marina to the center car where the fight with her father had taken place, the sleeping car now, most of the seats unbolted from the flooring and discarded before nightfall, the wooden parts burned in the locomotive's boiler. They found a corner of floorspace and, since there weren't enough blankets, Frost spread a clean fatigue blouse on the floor and lay down beside her. He felt her taking his hand and moving it to the zipper of the jeans she wore. He pulled down the zipper and pried the pants down past her hips, pulling a rain poncho over them then and taking her pants off the rest of the way. There were

163

panties, too, lace trimmed and feeling like silk to his rough hands there in the warm darkness. He pushed them down to where they clung only to her right ankle and her legs were free to curl around his back. He pulled his own pants down, but there'd been no time to actually undress, his boots still on, his chest and arms still sweat-covered from the heat of the locomotive and the tropical night.

He felt her hands searching his chest and abdomen, then in a moment her right hand making a fist around his penis. He drew her head back, his fingers knotted into the hair at the nape of her neck, then kissed her hard, crushing her mouth beneath his. He could feel her tongue, the tip, fiery hot, against his own. As he slipped inside her, arching her back upward and pressing her tighter against him, her legs tightened around him. He let her lie flat then, against the hard wood of the floor, the shirt all that was beneath her as he unbuttoned her blouse and pushed it up, then undid the bra that bound her soft full breasts, pushing it away too. She was moving beneath him, her hips arching in little circular motions against and around him. He locked his elbows, his arms straight, his body pushing against hers, in that one instant her body and his all that there was in the world to him—Aguillara-Garcia, Commacho, Ambassadore Pilchner, the terrorists, the mercenary soldiers he couldn't trust? It was meaningless, but then the instant was gone and he sank beside her, crowding away the thoughts and holding her in his arms, kissing her, but slowly now. How many minutes before he'd recall some job yet to do, a security check, going over the map to judge their distance, another look at the dwindling wood supply—would they have to awaken everyone and cannibalize more of the seats? For the moment, Frost thought absently, it could all wait. For the moment, and the moment only . . .

Chapter Fourteen

The whistling steam from the brakes clouded up
on both sides of the engine as Frost, on duty again,
ground the nineteenth-century locomotive to a
halt in the clearing. There were no water towers
and aside from taking on wood here it would be
necessary to form a bucket brigade and get water
for the locomotive from the stream some twenty-
five yards away. Pearblossom was back in the last
car already, forming a work brigade. Nearly out of
drinking water as well, some of the women, led by
Marina, would get water boiled from the stream

and then lace it with halazone tablets. The last of the fresh food had been consumed the previous night, but there were sufficient canned rations for use for another three days and, at the outside, as long as the train and the track held together, they would be on the road for another day at the most.

Frost swung out of the cab and down to the ground. The incessant chugging sound of the locomotive would not go away, even when he held his hands over his ears. He walked as far away as possible from the locomotive cab, walking back along the train to see if Pearblossom had the work party out yet.

Already, men with saws and axes from the foraging kits taken from the deuce-and-a-half trucks left behind were starting into the rain forest, long coils of rope shoulder-carried by some for hauling logs out to where they could be sawn apart. It was seven forty-five A.M. by the black face of Frost's Omega and he estimated that with luck and a lack of significant injuries, the forrestry operation would be over by noontime and they could be safely underway again by one P.M. Making the mental calculations, figuring that they would be going slowly because of the mountain looming up several miles ahead of them, he estimated they would reach Mexico by perhaps eight that night—several hours ahead of his original calculations because ever since dawn he'd been pushing the engine to near fifty miles per hour and almost halving their travel time over the nighttime hours.

Again, with Marina nearby to alert him this

time, Frost decided to try to catch some sleep. He'd collected perhaps four hours the previous night and none the night before. He sat on the ground by the last of the passenger cars, his scratched and dinged CAR-16 across his knees, the camouflage crusher hat down over his eye against the strong early morning sun. It was cooler than it had been the previous night and he no longer felt uncomfortable wearing a shirt. But as he gradually fell asleep under the sun, the thought kept nagging at him that there had been no contact with the terrorists or Commacho's army yet—no resistance at all since the attack near the airport fence as they had been leaving the city.

Frost had no idea how long he'd actually slept, but what awakened him was Marina's voice—he'd warned her not to come up on him and put a hand to his shoulder. The Viet Nam war aftermath had been full of cases of men, too steeled to staying alive, breaking their wife's collar bone or their daughter's arm when being gently aroused from a disturbed sleep.

"What is it?" he asked her, yawning.

"I let you sleep as long as I could. Pearblossom has come back with the men and they are loading the train with the firewood. The bucket brigade has already taken on all the water the locomotive can use. All should be ready for leaving soon."

He looked up at her and smiled. "Thanks for letting me rest," then reached up his hand and took hers, then got to his feet. As he stretched, getting the kinks out after the—he checked the Omega on his wrist—three hours of sleep in a sitting position, he heard a gunshot, then a scream.

Wheeling toward the sound, he saw Mrs. Cardon, the Ambassadore's secretary, hands to her face, falling down into the railbed, blood gushing from a head wound. "Terrorists!" Frost shouted, then grabbing Marina and pushing her up the steps into the nearest of the passenger cars, he broke into a run toward the locomotive. Already the gunfire was everywhere, coming from the jungle all around them. It had to be terrorists, he knew, and not in great force or else there would have been a frontal assault. For some reason he couldn't fathom their favorite technique.

"All aboard!" Frost shouted, then, "Pearblossom, get this sucker moving!" The words "Before one of the damned terrorists shoots into the locomotive and ruptures the boiler" were unspoken. Breaking from the tree cover around them at last, Frost could count at least a dozen terrorists, the unmistakable profiles of AK-47s in their hands, the black armbands on their fatigues, their symbol, unmistakable.

His CAR-16 at high port, he passed Pearblossom as the "engineer" ran toward the train, Frost's destination beyond the locomotive toward the tracks in front of it to see if Mrs. Cardon was somehow still alive. He came up alongside her, dropped down into the dirt and gravel by the tracks and telescoped out the CAR-16's stock, brought the assault rifle to his shoulder and started streaming bursts of 5.56mm solids into the closest group of terrorists. A glance to his right, between bursts, confirmed Mrs. Cardon's death—there was nothing left of her face that would have been even recognizably human. Firing with his left hand now, with his right hand he awkwardly dragged the body from the tracks, over the railing beside him and rolled it down off the road bed to the ground, the blood leaving a narrow red trail on the gravel.

Getting up to his knees, he collapsed the stock on the assault rifle and continued firing, backing up, then turning to run, then looking back again and firing, knocking out two terrorists coming toward him, their AK-47s blazing on full auto as though they had all the ammunition in the world.

Reaching the locomotive and swinging up into the cab, Frost pushed the magazine release on his weapon and rammed a fresh twenty-round magazine up the butt, then checked both sides of the train. Everyone—except for the half dozen or so bodies he could recognize littering the ground—seemed aboard and Frost shouted to Pearblossom, "All right, man—give her the gas or whatever and get us out of here!"

As the locomotive started moving, slowly, almost painfully, he heard Pearblossom shouting over the groaning of the engine—"Got company dead ahead."

Glancing in front of them, Frost leaned out the cab and started firing. There were a half dozen terrorists dragging a good-sized log across the tracks. "Punch through that!" he shouted to Pearblossom.

"All right, Captain—punch through I do."

170

Throttling it out, the locomotive seemed almost to leap ahead.

Frost still firing from one side of the engine, the locomotive crashed into the log and carried it along for a moment on the cow catcher and then with a thunderous crashing sound the log flew away, unable to resist the train's momentum. Frost's CAR-16 came up dry as they passed the terrorists running now beside the locomotive.

Ripping his Browning High Power from the leather under his shoulder Frost fired it twice into the face of one of the terrorists trying to clamber aboard, knocking him back.

"Behind me!" he heard Pearblossom shout, and as Frost wheeled he spotted a terrorist clambering up into the cab. Frost lashed out with his right foot, his combat boot catching the man full in the face and driving him back out of the cab to the ground. As Frost started to turn, he looked up and to his left—a terrorist was onto the coal car and leaping down toward him.

Both men crashed hard against the metal floor of the locomotive's cab, Frost's head cracking audibly against it. Fighting unconsciousness, Frost smashed upward at an angle with his right knee, catching the terrorist in the groin. Then sliding away and getting up to his knees, Frost hauled his right fist back and hammered it forward, smashing into the terrorist's nose and crushing it. Pulling himself to his feet, Frost lashed out with his left foot and sent the man sprawling backward.

Losing his balance a moment and falling back

toward the controls, Frost scanned the floor for his gun, seeing it but too far away to grab it. The terrorist was going for his pistol and Frost had none. Ripping the boot knife from the sheath just inside the waistband of his trousers, Frost hurtled the blade underhand like a dart and the knife shot forward, punching hard into the terrorist's chest. Frost threw himself forward and grabbed at the handle of the knife, wrenching it free, then driving it down into the terrorist's throat.

On his feet again, Frost reached down and grabbed up his CAR-16, sidestepped the body of the terrorist as he reloaded the assault rifle and looked out the locomotive and behind them. There were no other terrorists in sight, apparently the remainder of the attacking force now left far behind.

Pearblossom's left shoulder was wet with blood. "You hanging in there?" Frost asked.

"Yeah, I'll be cool."

Frost put his rifle down, bent over the body of the terrorist there on the floor of the cab and pulled out his knife, then rolled the body head over heels out the side of the speeding locomotive, saying to it, "Don't forget to write just as soon as you learn how, pal."

He turned back to Pearblossom and checked the man's shoulder—it was a flesh wound, but bleeding badly. "Climb back there and get in line for the doctor—if they didn't get him."

"Man, this is like some cowboy movie—you sure them terrorists don't scalp their victims?"

"Get out of here," Frost shouted good-naturedly

over the noise of the locomotive. As Pearblossom started up over the coal car, Frost spotted his Browning on the floor of the cab, bent and retrieved it. He kept his eye on Pearblossom until the man was out of sight, then he turned back to face the track ahead of him.

Already, the engine was straining as they started the climb into the foothills, but with the head of steam they'd gotten up to escape the terrorists they were still going faster than he would have thought possible on the grade. After a while, forcing himself to calm down, Frost lit a cigarette.

It was an hour and about six cigarettes later when Pearblossom returned, coming back across the coal car and dropping down into the cab, his shoulder bandaged, that side of his fatigue blouse cut away. "You okay, Pearblossom? I'm fine up here."

"Come back in two hours and spell me, all right, Captain?"

"You sure?" Frost asked him.

"Yeah, I'm just fine—a little peace and quiet up here'll do me good," Pearblossom said, lighting a cigarette of his own.

Frost started up over the edge of the coal car, then clambered across the woodpile—between the uneven footing and the wind it was dangerous going. Reaching the opposite end of the coal car, Frost climbed down then jumped across to the opposite platform, letting himself in through the doorway. A few of the Embassy people and one of his mercenaries were in the car but not Marina. He decided the doctor must have been using the

173

second car like an infirmary. He walked out the door of the first car, then looked up. Three of his mercenaries were waiting for him there, Fledgette, Bilstein and Nifkawitz, the CIA man.

"Freeze, man," Fledgette growled.

Standing stock still, Frost said, "What you guys up to?"

"Taking you out, mon Capitan—haha," Fledgette laughed.

"I don't like your sense of humor," Frost said. "Not one bit, as a matter of fact, Andrew." Frost snaked the butt of his rifle forward and into Fledgette's groin, then cracked the muzzle hard into the side of Fledgette's head. Already Nifkawitz was jumping toward Frost and he sidestepped. Wheeling, he punched the muzzle of his CAR-16 into Bilstein's stomach and pulled the trigger, the impact of the full auto burst, hurtling Bilstein from the platforms between the cars and out to the side of the train, but wrenching the rifle from Frost's hands as well.

Nifkawitz was clinging to the railing on the side of the platform and Frost slashed down in a knife edge blow with the side of his right hand across Nifkawitz's fingers, the CIA man loosening his grasp on the rail and almost falling away. As Frost wheeled again, Fledgette, his face covered with blood, was hammering down toward Frost's head with a Government .45. Sidestepping, Frost caught the impact on the side of his left shoulder. Already the boot knife was in Frost's hand and he raked it forward, into Fledgette's throat and up, cutting away a piece of the man's left ear.

Frost started to turn to finish Nifkawitz. Then, he saw it, tried to dodge it but couldn't. It was Craymer, one of the small hatchets from the foraging equipment slashing down in his right hand—Frost felt the edge of the pain, the blackness and then a heavy thudding against the front of his head and—then nothing. . . .

Chapter Fifteen

Frost opened his eye. The vision was blurred and he could barely see, but as he came fully to consciousness he could feel a myriad of sensations. His ribs were stiff where he'd been kicked, the front of his forehead hurt and his face somehow felt stiff and swollen. He couldn't move his hands—he felt something cold and metallic on the wrists there, handcuffs he thought. And he was naked. Looking down he could make out a heavy girth of chain around his abdomen. He was in a sitting position, chained up against something. For the moment he wasn't quite sure what.

Looking around, he could see he was in one of the passenger cars, but there was no motion, the train had apparently stopped. He could see nothing through the windows but darkness—guessing, he figured he'd been out for perhaps five hours, maybe longer. Turning his head awkwardly he could see Craymer, sitting across from him, smiling.

"Hey, Captain—you're awake. Someone whacks you with the butt end of an axe on the head, you really go to racking up them 'Zs'."

"Drop dead," Frost muttered. He realized full well it was a rather prosaic remark, but it was the best he could think of on the spur of the moment—his head was throbbing.

Craymer stood up and came forward. "No, you are going to drop dead, but not before you get played with a little and start screaming and begging us to kill you, sucker—and I mean sucker with a capitol S, baby."

Shoerdell came in then. Frost looked at him, saying, "You too, huh. Where's Nifkawitz?"

"He's with Santarelli guarding the rest of your guys, the Marines and everybody else." Then turning to Craymer, Shoerdell said, "Boss 'll be in in a few minutes. When I told him the man here was comin' around, he said don't start the fun yet—wait till he gets here."

Craymer walked over to Frost, lashed out with his left foot and caught Frost in the ribs, then turning to Shoerdell, said, "You mean I shouldn't do none of that?" Shoerdell and Craymer laughed,

177

Shoerdell walking over to Frost, bending down and punching Frost full in the mouth, the blow slamming Frost's head back against whatever it was he was chained to—he still couldn't tell.

Frost's mouth filled up with blood and his front teeth felt loose, but spitting the blood onto the floor by Shoerdell's feet, he cracked, "I don't think he wants you to do any of that either."

Shoerdell took a half step back and raised the butt of his rifle, then started bringing it down toward Frost's face. Powerless to move or defend himself, Frost could do nothing but watch.

"Hold it Shoerdell—knock it off!"

The rifle butt stopped inches from Frost's nose. Frost turned and stared in the direction of the voice. It was Ambassadore Pilchner, Frost's pistol stuffed in his trouser band, a CAR-16—Frost couldn't be sure if it was his or not—in his right hand held loosely by the pistol grip.

"Forgive me for not getting up," Frost said to Pilchner, adding, "I heard some tough guy say that in a movie."

"That wonderful sense of humor right to the end. I can see your epitaph now, Captain," Pilchner said, his mouth breaking into a big grin. "'He died with a smile on his lips.' Well, let's just see how long you keep smiling. First I'm going to tell you what I'm going to do to you, then I'm going to tell you why, and then if you're not too terribly bored—" and he paused seemingly for effect, his upper lip curling back in what in an animal would have been a snarl—"we're going to make you beg us to kill you—and maybe if you beg really well we'll do it.''

Frost watched as Pilchner came over to him, searched the room a moment and found a stool and then sat down, not three feet from Frost's battered face. "First of all, you may be a little disoriented. You're naked of course and handcuffed—that much I'm sure you can tell. You're handcuffed to—which you may not have noticed—one of the cast iron seat frames. That's bolted to the floor. The cuffs are maximum security cuffs, so I'm told that even if you know any tricks for getting out of regular handcuffs they won't work with these. The reason you are naked, Captain, is so we can torture you. You'll have no reason to attempt to be brave—there is nothing we want to find out, nothing we want you to do—except perhaps provide a night's entertainment.

"It's nearly eight P.M. now, and we have at least twelve hours before we'll let you die. Now if you were to sleep twelve hours, they could go by in no time at all. But twelve hours of continuous torture in a regular pattern calculated not to let you slip into unconsciousness or death will likely seem an eternity to you.''

Pilchner paused and lit a cigar, puffed at it vigorously a moment and then touched the glowing tip to Frost's bare thigh. Frost swept his left leg under the low stool and knocked Pilchner to the floor.

"Why weren't his legs bound? See to it!"

Shoerdell and Craymer came forward and grabbed Frost's ankles and pulled the belt from Frost's pants that lay on the floor and lashed it

179

around his ankles.

Bending his legs under him and pushing him down on his ankles they stepped back.

Again, Pilchner drew the stool close to Frost, sitting down and touching the glowing tip of the cigar to Frost's chest this time and keeping it there, Frost gritting his teeth against the pain, then finally crying out. "That's much better, Captain," Pilchner said. "Now you're catching the spirit of the thing. I inflict the pain until you please me by reacting properly, then we can move on to explore new frontiers together."

"What nuthouse they get you out of?" Frost's voice was strained but he kept it even, under control but barely.

"Tsk, Captain Frost! In a few moments—short moments compared to the long, interminably long ones which will follow—you'll find out that you shouldn't be disrespectful to the man who dishes out the pain. That can have bad results, Captain."

Frost had always felt every man had a right to be what he wanted, do what he wanted and for that reason saw respecting the rights of homosexuals as fully compatible with his own live and let live philosophy. Pilchner, on the other hand, Frost now realized, was a homosexual but perhaps didn't even consciously realize it. The eyes staring at him, the almost quivering lips as Pilchner talked about the pain he had in store for Frost. And Frost could do nothing.

"At any event, Captain," Pilchner went on, "we are going to employ a technique proven most interesting supposedly by the Peronist Government torturers—electricity, drowning, beating and then more of the same. First, we wrap your body with wet cloths—we have some rags that will do nicely. Then we apply the electricity. I'm afraid we have no electrodes, but copper wire from the charged storage batteries out of the jeep will have to do. The damp towels around your body serve to step up the effect of the electric shock on your skin. Then, when you have had our fill of that, we immerse your head for prolonged periods in cold water—the colder the better really, but I'm afraid the tepid water from the drinking supply will have to do. Then, when you are gagging from the water you swallow, we pull you out and beat your abdomen with boards we've pried out of the floor here, beat it until you vomit out all the water you have swallowed. Then we start over again with the electricity, then the drowning, then the beating and vomiting, then the electricity again. If it's done skillfully, it can go on for more than a day without you once passing out. And believe me, I'll try my best, Captain."

"Why?" Frost said, the fear in his voice something he couldn't disguise anymore.

"Why? Well, as you probably guessed, I'm not acting out government policy. The Government is too stupid. State Department, the CIA—all of them are fools. Myself and the men in Washington—some in government, some in business, whom I represent simply feel that a Communist takeover in Latin America is inevitable and that the sooner the United States realizes this the better we all will be—and the less chance of a head-to-head nuclear confrontation with the Soviet Union. You might say I'm working for world peace. And the key to that is Mexico, Captain Frost. Sunny Mexico. And the key to Mexico was Monte Azul. That's why I ordered Aguillara-Garcia's brother liquidated in Switzerland, before he could consummate his arms deal, then hire you.

"Once Monte Azul finally falls and the anachronisms like Commacho are killed off and the demagogues like Aguillara-Garcia are in the people's prisons rather than preaching right wing philosophy, then Mexico cannot be far behind. And, with a Soviet dominated country on its southern border, the United States could not hope to do anything but give in to the inevitable."

"What about Aguillara-Garcia and his daughter, his wife?" Frost's mind was racing and he was trying to stall, but he didn't know for what. Once the torture started, he knew what he had to do.

"They, along with all the Marines, your mercenaries who were loyal to you—like Pearblossom, for example—and all the Embassy staff will be captured by the terrorists—they'll be here by eight tomorrow morning. I will miraculously escape to tell the story of how you kidnapped Aguillara-Garcia, handed him over to the terrorists in barter for your own life, then had some sort of mysterious falling out—perhaps over money. They tortured you horribly then put a bullet into your brain. You do have a brain, Captain? Humor," Pilchner said. "I thought you'd like that."

Frost forced a smile.

After a moment, Pilchner sitting there quietly staring at him, Frost said, "Can I ask one question? Seriously, before you ah—"

"Get started? Yes, ask anything you like, Captain."

"Why the torture, why not just kill me?"

"That's a very fair question, Captain. And my answer is a simple one. I sincerely hate you and most sincerely think I'll enjoy every beautiful minute of your agony. Why don't we begin? I think the copper wires around the testicles and on the nipples of your breasts would be the most logical place to start, don't you? Later on we can move to the tongue. I understand the sensation of high voltage there is quite extraordinary."

Chapter Sixteen

They'd wrapped Frost in the wet rags and despite the heat of the night, the dampness against his naked skin and the fear he couldn't help but feel were making him shiver. Like a mummy, his ankles, knees and thighs bound with rope, his wrists still cuffed and his arms pinioned behind him with heavy ropes, he could barely move a major muscle independently. They forced him down into a kneeling position resting on his heels and then poured buckets of water onto him until he almost choked.

Already, he could see the storage batteries they had brought in with the long copper wires attached to them. All three of his torturers wore rubber gloves to guard themselves against the shock.

Shoerdell seemed to be having fun, making the copper wires spark when he touched them together. About to begin, Pilchner took a balled up oily rag from the floor and stuffed it into Frost's mouth, saying, "We wouldn't want you to bite your tongue off, would we?" The smell of the oil was making Frost start to gag. He tried moving his tongue around to catch the end of the rag and swallow it to make himself choke, but could not. He knew he had to endure the first bout of the electric shock torture and still keep his wits about him. That way when it came time to immerse his head in the water he could swallow huge gulps, breathe it in and finish himself, cheating them of their night of thrills.

For a moment, as they poured the last bucket of water over him and dragged the largest of the dry cell batteries toward him so the wires would reach, he thought of Bess and that he would never see her again, and of Marina, Aguillara-Garcia's daughter. He hoped somehow she'd manage to escape a firing squad, but he could not see how.

Shoerdell started to take the copper wires and wind them around Frost's testicles, but Pilchner grabbed the wires from him and said, "No—I want to." Frost could feel Pilchner's hands there and they stayed longer than they should have—to Frost this was the worst of the torture, worse by far he felt

185

than what was to come.

But then he realized in an instant that he had been horribly wrong. How could he have been so wrong he asked himself, for the electricity was burning at him and his body was twitching uncontrollably, each muscle burning and feeling as though it would rip apart from him, the focus of pain his testicles where the electricity was entering his body. He screamed even through the oily rag balled into his mouth, heard Pilchner, clearly saying, "Oh, good. Listen to that scream, would you? Fantastic—fantastic! Try it with a second battery before we move on—make him jump."

And Frost jumped, flapping around on the floor, Shoerdell hardly able to keep up with the rolling and pitching of the electricity through his body. Frost's head slammed against the far wall and he almost went out, but then the electricity stopped for a moment. It was Shoerdell's voice through the haze of pain and nausea. "Hey, you know, man, this is all right. What I'm gonna do here is hook the wires from the batteries to the wire around his testicles—worst that can happen is he jumps so hard he castrates himself, but we can still keep him alive long enough to have some more fun."

Frost felt the hands at his testicles, the wire cutting into his skin, then the electricity again and he could feel nothing but pain everywhere in his body. He knew he was flopping around on the floor of the car like a dying fish on the sand but there was nothing he could do. When his head hit into the floor or a wall he could barely notice any difference in the level of pain.

Then the electricity stopped, but by now there was little difference in the pain—only the flopping around on the floor stopped for Frost. He felt the wires being attached with alligator clips through the wet cloth covering his chest, the pain of the clips a new sensation of intensity and disgust, self-loathing that somehow he couldn't make himself die. He tried to swallow the rag again but still could not get the end of it. Then the current came and he felt himself lifting off the floor and hammering down against it, again and again and then there was only blackness and he hoped he was dead.

"Captain Frost?" he heard Pilchner's voice cooing. "You passed out on us."

He could feel Pilchner's hand in his hair, opened his eye and saw the trough of water in front of him and silently said, "Thank God." As they pressed his face under the water, involuntarily he closed his mouth and inhaled, then cursed himself for it, forcing the air out of his nose, opening his mouth and drinking in the merciful, death-giving brackish water.

But in a moment his head was out of the water again and he was on his back staring up at the improvised barebulb light swinging over him, and the beating started. His stomach, his ribs, the pressure, the pain was unbearable and then after a while it didn't seem to matter anymore. He heard Pilchner's voice—the voice of his torturer, the one who gave the pain—saying, "Tried to drown yourself—I knew you would but I expected it so we pulled you out in time. In a moment, after we're through beating the boards against you until you vomit, we'll begin with the electricity again. I liked that. Did you?"

Frost threw up, all over himself and the floor and then rolled over when they stopped beating him, his face in the mess he'd made.

"Do the electricity again," he heard Pilchner cooing and in a moment the gag was in his mouth and the wires were on him and the current was ripping through his chest, through his crotch. And all time was gone as he flapped and rolled and screamed and tried desperately to swallow the rag and choke to death but couldn't.

He opened his eye, this time his head already under the water—"Where had the time gone?" he asked himself. And he tried swallowing the water and they pulled him out and beat at him again and again he threw up, but it was only water something at the back of his mind told him. And then the electricity again and by now Frost didn't care, the pain so constant and horrifying that it didn't matter—he only wanted them through with him so he could die. The water—he could see it in front of him—

"Batardo!" It was a woman's voice, Spanish?

The rag was out of his mouth, Frost realized. Why couldn't he speak. Had they put the electrodes to his tongue yet? He couldn't remember.

"Batardo," he heard again. Marina? A gunshot, two more, then a burst of automatic weapons fire. Then Pilchner's voice saying, "Please, Senorita Aguillara-Garcia—no, don't kill me. Please. Nifkawitz—what are you doing?'' There was a loud cracking sound. Frost tried raising his head from the trough of water and could not, but sank into it instead. ''Thank God,'' he thought, ''I'm going to die.''

He felt his head pulled out of the water, gentle hands, a woman's hands unwinding the copper wire from him, pulling the rags from his body.

He lay in the corner, naked, a blanket over him for long minutes, a cigarette dangling from his mouth, his pistol clutched in his right hand like a talisman. After a while he became aware of the fact that Marina was talking to him. ''Hank, are you all right—can we do something?'' He remembered answering that same question several years earlier, he thought. ''Yes, I'll be all right. Just let me get my breath, okay.''

She'd given him his watch and he could see straight finally and read it. He remembered Pilchner saying it was nearly eight just before the torture had gotten started and his watch now read well after eleven.

Frost stared at Pilchner, sitting in the corner, legs folded, hands clasped behind his head, a bruise darkening at his jaw. Nifkawitz had one of the submachine guns leveled at Pilchner's gut.

''Where's Pearblossom?'' The evenness of his own voice astounded Frost.

Nifkawitz said, ''He's guarding the two guys who were guarding all of us. Why, you want him? I can send Marina.''

''No,'' Frost said, his voice still calm, ''but thanks very much. Listen, I really don't know how

189

to repay you and Marina for this—seriously." The evenness of his own voice almost frightened Frost now. He decided that he was no longer sane.

"Say, could either of you get me another cigarette—I'd really like that."

"Hank?" It was Marina's voice. "Are you sure you are all right?"

"Listen, kid, fine I tell you. I'm going to kill that evil son of a bitch now. So Marina, I wouldn't watch this. Please." Frost stood up. His legs were shakey and halfway to the corner of the railroad car he remembered he was naked. Marina came toward him with a blanket and he smiled and gently pushed her away.

There was a machete there in the corner, from one of the foraging kits, he thought. Frost picked it up and started walking the long distance toward Pilchner. How many miles was it he thought, had to be quite a lot.

"Stand up, Mr. Ambassadore—please," he heard himself saying and Pilchner stood, his hands trembling, a dark stain starting in the front of his pants. Awkwardly not letting go of his pistol, Frost remembered taking the machete in a full baseball batlike swing with both hands and the sound it made cutting through the air was a long, loud, "whoosh," and the sound of Pilchner's head hitting the wooden floor was like the sound of a coconut falling from a palm tree.

Palm trees sway before they fall, Frost thought. Then he swayed and he fell.

Frost opened his eye, his head in Marina's lap, he guessed, because all he could see was her face, and he had no idea where he was. So he asked her, "Where am I, I mean where on the train or whatever?"

"Shh, Hank. We cleared out the front car so we are all alone now, just you and I—you've been sleeping."

"I need some aspirin—I'm sorry you saw me kill Pilchner."

"He deserved it."

"Yeah," Frost said, "can't argue with that I guess. Do you guys know about the terrorists coming tomorrow in the morning, or today in the morning—I don't know what time it is. Help me up."

"Hank," she said, "you're too disconnected."

"I don't have to be intelligent for a while, just look that way. Come on, get me up."

"No, Hank!"

"Yes, Marina."

"No, please."

"Come on, dammit," Frost said, then started pulling himself to his feet.

"You can't, the doctor hasn't even seen you yet. He's still working on the people who were wounded when Ambassadore Pilchner took over the train."

"I don't need a doctor—at least not for anything that can be fixed." He stood up and, like a child almost, he had to be helped getting dressed because his hands shook too badly. Like a bullfighter, getting ready for a Sunday afternoon waltz with death, Frost was helped into his shoulder holster and now finally, he released the grip he had on the

Browning High Power, having even held it in his hand along with the machete when he had killed Pilchner, he remembered.

His web trouser belt was gone and he had Marina go out for a moment and find him another. The knife in place, the shoulder harness in place and the CAR-16—Pilchner had been using his—in his hands, Frost felt almost whole again, except for the unnatural feeling between his legs, the uncertainty and sometimes the horrible certainty that what Pilchner and the other torturers had done had somehow robbed him of—He wouldn't verbalize the thought.

Every muscle in his body ached, his head throbbed despite the aspirin he'd taken but he wouldn't risk anything stronger, the few hours remaining before daylight—it was four-thirty—were too vital.

Nifkawitz was standing guard outside and Frost stepped down from the railroad car and went over to him, the coolness of the night air making Frost shiver. "Thanks," Frost muttered.

"You got a cigarette?" the CIA man said.

"Yeah, how about a right arm too, I mean it, thanks," Frost said, handing his pack of Camels over, then getting it back and letting Nifkawitz light his cigarette as well—his hands were still trembling too badly.

"You gonna make it—I mean Pearblossom can still run the locomotive, and I figure you probably guess you can trust me."

"Yeah—I trust you," Frost admitted. "Obviously, now. But I'm not out for that, we have to get this train going as fast as we can. There should be a major terrorist force here by dawn, and I'll bet General Commacho's people aren't far behind them—we could wind up the object of everyone's disaffection in a three-way battle and this train has its limits."

"How far you figure we are from Mexico. I mean I can count on us getting help there. The Mexican authorities have been tipped."

"That's good to know," Frost told him. "Maybe about four hours of pushing it—six hours at the most. You and Pearblossom make sure everybody who should be is aboard, get everyone who can shoot something to shoot with and then have Pearblossom get this thing rolling. Take whatever men I've got left and the remainder of the Marine detachment and get 'em on top of the train, but keeping low. You sit like fly paper with Aguillara-Garcia and his wife. I'll be with Marina—I gotta check something out."

As Frost turned away, he heard Nifkawitz's voice behind him. "Hey, I know better than to say something about the girl, but I'm just talking about you, now. Good luck, man." Frost just stood there a moment, then nodded, not knowing if Nifkawitz could see him in the pale yellow light coming from the window of the coach car or not.

Frost went back inside the car—like before, just Marina was there. She sat crosslegged on a stack of blankets, one of the blankets wrapped around her just covering her breasts. "Come here, Hank, I know what you must feel."

Frost walked toward her, put down his rifle and

dropped to his knees beside her, felt her hands reaching out and unbuttoning his fatigue blouse. He didn't move for a moment. "Forget it," he said.

"No," she whispered. "I want to—for both of us, Hank. What if this is the last morning we live?"

He took her in his arms then and held her and after a few moments, the rumbling of the train starting beneath them as it clicked over the rails, Frost lay down beside Marina, his lips finding hers, their hands exploring each other's bodies, hers gentle against him.

He was worrying too hard about it, he knew. She kissed him hard on the mouth and without thinking he responded, her body pressed against him, her abdomen arched into his. Very suddenly, he closed his eye, whispered to her that she was beautiful and, despite the pain it gave him this first time after the torture session, Frost exploded inside of her. Her hand resting against his chest, the warmth and feeling back in him again, he stared at the darkness of the ceiling until something else, perhaps equally as strong as a sex drive, returned to him—the knowledge that his job was not finished.

Chapter Seventeen

"You look a hell of a lot better, man."

Frost turned to Nifkawitz, then turned and looked down at the sleeping form of President Aguillara-Garcia. "Doc says he's comin' along fine," Nifkawitz said.

"Good. You're going to be on duty here until we get into Mexico—you ever find out who the other CIA guy was?"

"Yeah, it was Pearblossom all along. Man, that I would never have figured."

"Good man regardless of who he works for—

I'm goin' up forward. When the shooting starts—I know it will—we're going to push this thing as fast as she'll go. Remember, your job isn't defense of the train, it's defense of Aguillara-Garcia—don't forget."

Frost continued walking through, then stopped. Anna, the President's wife, was sitting alone in the opposite corner of the car. Unslinging the CAR-16, Frost walked over toward her. "How you doin', Anna?"

"He is sending me away if we reach Mexico alive—he told me that. Marina spoke with him. He already knew about you having an affair with her, and it did not bother him. He likes you." She turned her face away from him.

"The gentlemanly thing to say is, I'm sorry. At least I suppose that's what I should say." Frost lit a cigarette and offered her one. She took it. His hands rock-steady again, he lit it for her with the Zippo he carried.

"And you, Capitan Frost, are you well now after your ordeal? Rumors were going through the passengers here, that they tortured you badly."

"That's true enough," Frost said. "I'll make it—stiff as hell though," he added, smiling. She smiled back at him.

"Via con Dios, Capitan—I mean that."

He took her outstretched hand—the fallen woman, and she played the part well, she was still handling it better than he'd thought. "Can I give you some advice?" he asked.

"Si," she whispered.

"All these years you've been working on the idea

196

that you needed to club someone into your bed. Maybe all you needed to do was be yourself," and he bent down and kissed Anna lightly on the lips, snatched up his rifle from the seat beside her and walked through the doorway onto the platform.

He jumped, stiffly, onto the next car, then climbed the cast iron ladder to the roof. Two of the Marines were up top, faced in either direction, both men prone. As he walked past them, precariously keeping his balance as the car bumped beneath him, one of them turned and looked up at him, "Good morning, sir. How are you feeling?"

Frost glanced at the insignia on the man's uniform. "Fine, Corporal, thank you. I'll make it." Then changing the subject, "Any sign of the enemy?"

"No, sir, but they could be out there a hundred yards or so into the jungle."

Frost glanced down at his watch, his body swaying with the motion of the train. "We should be entering the mountains in less than an hour, so they won't have any jungle left to hide in," he said. Giving the men a nod, he continued forward, climbed down to the platform opposite the coal car, then jumped across, his muscles burning as he climbed atop the coal car and made his way over the ridges of firewood then down the other side into the locomotive cab.

Pearblossom, startled, turned around, his right hand on a Government Model .45 Colt. His face broke into a smile, though, as Frost came toward him. "How you doin', Captain?"

197

Frost smiled, sticking out his right hand and clasping Pearblossom on the shoulder. "Thanks for helping Marina and Nifkawitz last night—I owe you a lot."

"When's the punch line?"

Frost just shook his head and lit a cigarette. "I was serious, man."

"Well, listen, Captain. I mean you know about my thing with CIA now and all, but nothin' last night was gonna make me let them do what they was doin' to ya' any longer than I could help it— you know, we started hearing this hollerin' and all a little after eight o'clock and it just kept on comin' and comin'. You got balls, man."

"Almost lost them though," Frost remarked, staring at the rain forest thinning out now on both sides as they climbed toward the mountains.

"Yeah, well anyway," Pearblossom said, noticeably uncomfortable with the conversation, "I'm glad you're doin' okay, Captain."

"Right, enough said."

"When you expectin' our company?"

Frost lit another cigarette, then said, "Well, I checked with the map and there's a ten- or twelve-mile-long canyon we pass through once we get up into the mountains, then down the other side is Mexico. Since the terrorists didn't catch us this morning early, they shouldn't be more than say two hours behind us, maybe with helicopters to carry them. They'll go for us in the canyon, I figure. And before we got rolling this morning, I walked back down the line a little and did some thinking. I figure if Commacho knows where we are the smartest thing for him to have done would be to get a fast train and go after us. He couldn't risk a helicopter assault force coming down on us and Aguillara-Garcia getting killed. I don't know for a fact, but he's a smart enough old campaigner that he could be waiting for that canyon too—there's a six percent grade or so according to the topographic map, which means we'll be going awful slow, but a more modern train wouldn't have to."

"Why don't we just stop and whack out the tracks behind us—derail him?"

"Two reasons," Frost said. "If the terrorists do overtake us, Commacho may be the only hope we have of saving Aguillara-Garcia—our primary job. I'll be dead as a doornail but that's nothin' I can do anything to change—I'd be dead if the terrorists got us too. And at least with Commacho, you and Nifkawitz and the Embassy people wouldn't get killed."

"What's the second reason, Captain?" Pearblossom asked.

"Even though Commacho is out after us, he's still a friendly force—I just have a bad gut level reaction to wiping out anywhere from a couple dozen to a couple hundred of his men. With Commacho gone, Monte Azul woudn't even hold together long enough for anybody who was anti-Communist to get out alive—men, women, kids—the whole routine."

"Yeah," Pearblossom said, almost sadly. "You think we did the right thing? Now like I was following orders from the Company—'Help get

Aguillara-Garcia to safety.' You know. But you can't pass the moral buck."

Frost looked at Pearblossom for a second, then looked away, watching the rails up ahead of them, the train pouring on the speed to prevent the terrorists behind them from getting in front of them and setting up a derailment of their own. "I gave up a long time ago trying to figure out what's right in international relations. Were you in Viet Nam?"

"Yeah, I try real hard to forget about it, though," Pearblossom sighed.

"Like I said before," Frost said, his voice low, "enough said."

The day dragged on toward noon and by the time the sun had climbed that high, the train had left the rain forest fully behind, for the barren granite rock faces of the mountains and the ever-steepening grade. To keep up any speed at all, the boiler had to be cranking as much steam as possible and that had already started a serious drain on the wood supply. Frost had left Pearblossom, the more competent engineer, at the locomotive's controls and gone off to organize a work party from among the Embassy staff, the surviving Marines and his few mercenaries—a work party to cannibalize everything possible that would burn to keep the boiler cooking. The wooden ammunition boxes were among the last to go, and Frost solved the logistical problem of where to store the ammo simply by issuing all of it to anyone who could fire a gun. All of Pilchner's men were dead, and Frost had no choice but to work on the assumption that everyone remaining aboard the train could be trusted.

A human conveyor belt was formed to ferry the wood to the coal car through the three passenger cars. Walking through the center car where the torture session had taken place still gave Frost the chills. For an hour, Frost relieved Nifkawitz in his watch over Aguillara-Garcia, then once Nifkawitz had returned Frost started forward to the locomotive again. Marina was working in the forward portion of the first car as he passed the line of destroyed chairs, doors and packing crates. She walked with him to the only quiet corner of the forward car. "What is it?" Frost asked her.

"Do you think we are going to make it through, Hank?"

He glanced down at his watch. "We'll be entering the canyon up ahead in about five minutes—that's why I'm going forward now. If by some miracle we get through there, then we'll make it. The worst that could happen then would be Commacho's troops somehow intercepting us. So, I can't answer your question. If the shooting does start, stay with your father and Nifkawitz and do what you can from there. You know how to handle a gun?"

"I have shot trap many times, so I know how to fire a shotgun. That is all."

"Well," he said, "we don't have any shotguns— almost wish we did. Just take a CAR-16 or M-16 and point it and shoot—after a few rounds it'll come to you. Leave it on semi-automatic to save on going through a full magazine the first time you touch the trigger—that always happens the first time anyone gets on full-automatic. You'll be fine."

Frost leaned toward her and kissed her mouth lightly, then felt her coming into his arms. As he kissed her, over his shoulder he could see some of the Embassy people staring, but anyone who was aboard the train and didn't know that Frost and Marina were lovers, Frost thought just wasn't paying attention.

As Frost started to move away, Marina touched his arm, saying, "Be careful, Hank."

He looked at her and smiled. "You realize what a superfluous statement that is—'be careful.' What do you think I'm going to do? Be reckless? Don't worry." Then, with a great deal more confidence than he felt, Frost added, "You just relax, kid, I'll be fine." He squeezed her hand and gave her a wink, then caught up his rifle from the corner and started forward through the car. As Frost reached the platform, dodging half a wooden seat back, he looked up. Two things immediately caught his attention.

The train was well along into the entrance of the canyon, ever-steepening sheer rock face rising on each side now, the base of the walls perhaps fifty yards at the greatest distance on each side of the train. And, on the top of the right hand canyon wall, Frost had caught the glint in the sunlight of a sniper scope.

Wheeling, he shouted into the car, "Everybody get to cover—now!"

Hitching the CAR-16 across his back, he started

up the iron ladder toward the roof of the car, as soon as his head broke over the edge shouting to the defenders up top, "Company on the canyon walls—spotted a sniper scope—wait for them to open fire and keep low!"

Frost slid down the ladder, hands skidding on the parallel vertical supports, then jumped across from the platform to the coal car and clambered up to the top. Midway across it, he shouted to Pearblossom, "Give her everything she's got, Herb. The shooting 'll start any second."

Pearblossom looked around, gave Frost a nod and punched the throttle. Frost glanced back behind them along the side of the train. As their own train rounded a curve taking them fully into the canyon, he just barely caught sight of another train behind them—the flag of the Army of Monte Azul flapping on both sides of the engine.

It was Commacho. Frost said to himself, "Hell and damnation."

Chapter Eighteen

The Government troop train with Commacho in command was behind them, the terrorists were ranked on both rims of the narrow canyon through which they passed.

Staring behind them, Frost could see the military train clearly now as it too rounded the final curve into the canyon. It was a modern train, traveling quite noticeably faster than they were. Standing in a half crouch on the woodpile of the coal car, Frost gave a silent nod to his "amigo" Commacho, because what Frost knew now that he must do might well cause the man's death.

The terrorists would not be dissuaded by the presence of the troop train. Whereas with the train Frost rode they wanted to stop it to take prisoners, to capture Aguillara-Garcia and give him a "trial," there was no such reasoning that would apply to Commacho's train. They would attempt to destroy and from their superior position on the rim of the canyon, that would be piteously easy.

"Keep pouring it on," Frost shouted to Pearblossom, for the train if anything seemed to be going more slowly. Frost looked ahead of them— the tracks were climbing steeply. If there were a rockslide or other barricade ahead of them along the tracks, Frost doubted the engine would have the momentum to push it off the tracks.

He clambered down, back toward the first passenger car. Frost ripped open the door—it had been left in place unlike the other passenger doors simply to cut down on the smoke and soot from being positioned directly behind the woodburning engine. He shouted to Marina, "Get somebody running back through the cars—I want everybody into this first car as quickly as possible, then have someone get the shooters off the roofs of the last two cars—hurry!"

Still, as he looked back toward the canyon rim, there was no shooting. What were they waiting for? He could even see large groups of the terrorists following along as best they could, along the top of the canyon wall.

He closed his eye a moment—he hadn't been thinking clearly, he realized. He knew their plan.

In his mind, he visualized the topographic map—the suspension bridge at the end of the canyon. "My God," he whispered slowly. Shouting "Hurry," then leaping across to the coal car, he clambered frantically to the top.

Frost lost his balance and started to slip, then catching himself moved forward. At the lip of the coal car closest to the locomotive cab, Frost shouted across to Pearblossom, "I know why they haven't opened fire yet—there's a bridge maybe two miles ahead of us—they want us pouring on the speed and coming out of the canyon as fast as we can. The engine, maybe the first car behind the coal car—they'd just dive right over into the gorge. You gotta start slowing down—now. I'm releasing those last two cars into Commacho's train. It'll maybe derail them but otherwise their train 'll slam right into us and this whole thing will go."

Frost thought he heard Pearblossom yelling at him over the noise of the locomotive, "Good luck!"

Already, Frost could feel the train under him starting to slow, hear the wheels starting to skid against the track they rode. There was no time for going over the roofs of the cars—it would be faster going through the cars, he reasoned.

Already, too, with the train slowing however slightly, the terrorists were starting to open fire, mortar fire raining down on the train from the lip of the canyon, that and heavy machinegun and small arms fire. Bullets were whizzing about Frost as he jumped down from the coal car to the passenger car platform, then pushed through the door. "Everybody down unless you can return fire—and brace yourselves for a fast stop," Frost shouted.

As he ran through the already crowded front car, he scanned the faces there for Marina's but couldn't find it. He pushed his way against the crowds coming in from the second car, gunfire again trained on him from the canyon rim as he crossed from car to car. The aisle was crowded and he clambered around the few remaining seats, pushing his way toward the rear of the second car. Still, there was no sign of Marina anywhere. He reached the door, then pushed past the last stragglers and entered the last car. Marina was not there, and the car was otherwise empty.

If he hadn't somehow missed her, Frost realized, it was either that she'd taken a round and fell from the train or for some reason she was on one of the car roofs.

Frost was under heavy fire now, but climbing the ladder toward the roof of the last car there was no chance to use his own weapons to return fire. He looked back along the roof of the last car—no one was there.

Despairing, he shot a glance forward. Near the center on the roof of the second car he saw Marina, the view freezing itself in his consciousness like some frightening photograph. Her left arm was dripping blood and she was on her knees beside the body of one of the Marines, trying to move him.

"Marina!" Frost shouted at her, but the rush of wind was going against his voice and he realized

207

the futility of crying out to her. The gunfire was heavier now, from both sides, greater concentrations of terrorist troops on both rims pouring it down, chunks of wood from the passenger car roofs ripping up under the impact of bullets striking all about him. Ahead, along the roofline, he saw a curve. Was it the curve just before the bridge? he asked himself. It had to be.

No time to be careful, he took a few steps back along the roof of the last car then ran forward, jumping the five feet or so between the cars and coming down hard on his knees on the roof of the second car. Dragging himself to his feet he ran forward in a low crouch, a slug ripping a flesh wound across his back and making him stumble forward. He got up again, then made it the last few feet to Marina and the young Marine she was trying to save. Useless though he knew it to be, there, crouched beside the girl and the fallen Marine, Frost opened up toward the nearest of the canyon rims with his CAR-16, then snatched up the M-16 from the Marine and this in his left hand started firing both assault rifles at once, firing until both had come up empty. He tossed the M-16 away and slung the CAR across his back. Marina was paralyzed with fear. Frost bent down beside her and slapped her, "Come on—help me! I've got to get you down from here."

There was no sense in taking her back the way he'd come—somehow he still had to get to the couplings and loosen these last two cars. He dragged her to her feet, keeping her down in a low crouch. Suddenly, her eyes welled up with tears.

"Hank!" she screamed. With her helping now, Frost grabbed the young Marine, moaning even though unconscious, then started hauling him across the roof. Halfway to the edge Frost gave up, shouting to Marina, "Go ahead—get into that first car and get someone to help me get him down!"

She ran forward, fighting to keep her balance against the sway of the train. As Frost bent over to drag the 180-pound Marine onto his shoulder, he glanced ahead. They were into the curve now and a mile or so away he could see the bridge—what was left of it—and the gorge yawning up waiting for them to fall in.

The Marine over his shoulder, fighting to keep from being pitched over the side, Frost started forward. He felt slugs hammering into the body partially covering his.

As he reached the edge of the roof, he saw hands—Nifkawitz disobeying orders again and again Frost was happy he had. Frost dropped hard to his knees and slid the body of the young Marine down onto the platform, then tossing his rifle across the airspace to Nifkawitz, he shouted, "Brace yourselves in there—we're gonna crash."

Turning, he started running back across the roof of the second car. He could hear the screeching from the locomotive far forward of him, the wheels reversing to stop the train—all trace of a grade seemingly gone now, the engine speeding along the straightaway toward disaster.

Midway across the second car, Frost went down, a slug tearing into his left thigh. He pulled himself to his feet again and kept going. At the far edge of the second car he started for the ladder, a fusillade of machinegun fire eating away the edge of the roofline. He dove down to the platform, coming down hard against his left shoulder, the bullet wounds across his shoulder blades and in his left thigh starting to pain him badly.

Reaching down, pulling himself across to the second car as he did, he struggled with the coupling. It wouldn't budge. The strongest tool he had was the boot knife. Using it as a pry against the hinge pin, the tool steel blade snapped, but the pin was up enough that Frost was able to free it. The Commacho troop train was less than two hundred yards behind them and Frost watched as the car followed along for an instant and then started to roll backwards, slowly at first, then gathering up speed. As Frost limped through the second car toward the final coupling, he silently thanked God there had been enough of an incline left for his plan to work. He reached the last platform. As he started through the doorway, a torrent of gunfire began raining down on him. The terrorists on the rim of the canyon could see his plan and wanted to prevent it, Frost realized.

Frost pushed through the door and leaped across to the platform of the leading car, a bullet searing across his left wrist as he did. He glanced down—there was barely any blood, the wound like a large razor cut.

Almost ripping away the flesh from his fingertips, Frost pulled on the final hinge pin. It wouldn't budge. He used what was left of his boot knife and pried. It started to move. His fingernails breaking against it, Frost heaved against the pin. It was free. Tossing the pin aside, he watched as the second car started back, following the first on a collision course with Commacho's train. The screeching of the wheels reversing against the track beneath him was louder now and as Frost dove through the door to the comparative safety of the coach car, the impact came.

Frost started falling forward, then stopped in mid-fall as though some invisible hand—the force of the collision—had caught him and pushed him back. He hit against the doorway, hard, the wood shattering behind his body, his left shoulder taking it full-force.

Suddenly there was no motion at all. Shaking his head to clear it, Frost hauled himself to his feet and started forward as fast as he could move. Reaching the forward door closest to the coal car, he wrenched it open and looked through.

The coal car and the rear half of the engine were still on the track, the front half of the engine hanging in air suspended over the edge of the sabotaged bridge.

Glancing around them, Frost spotted what the locomotive had hit—the piled-up ties from the track put across the bridge, placed to block the train and slow it enough to keep the whole thing from going over the side. Frost smiled ruefully— the terrorists wanted Aguillara-Garcia as badly as he had thought.

"Pearblossom!" he shouted.

"My leg," Frost heard Pearblossom shouting back feebly.

Frost started through the doorway. "You'll be killed," Marina, beside him suddenly, screamed.

He turned to her. "Did you, Nifkawitz or Pearblossom think about your own necks very much last night?" Smiling at her, then turning away, he let the question go unanswered. Once through the door, the gunfire resuming now, he glanced behind the car before climbing across to the coal car.

He could faintly hear the sound of Commacho's train, could still see the last of the two cars he'd released slowly going back down the grade. And as he watched, it happened. There was an ear-splitting crack, a fireball shooting up thirty or more feet into the air, then another, even louder crashing sound, then an explosion and a second fireball, this unimaginably huge, towering almost to the very rim of the canyon. And then Frost could see nothing more, for where the engine of Commacho's train had been there was nothing but a wall of flame and thick black smoke.

"Buenas suerte—good luck," Frost said under his breath to Commacho. Again the terrorist gunfire from both sides of the rim of the canyon picked up, but heedless of it Frost stepped across to the coal car, clambered up the side then made his way across.

As Frost started down the other side of the coal car, he could see Pearblossom and he could see why Pearblossom was trapped. The rear face of the boiler had blown into the cab and Pearblossom's left leg was lost beneath it, hot coals littered across the floor. As Frost awkwardly jumped down to the cab, he could see Pearblossom's face—it was scalded by the steam from the exploding boiler. The eyes were staring up blankly toward the ceiling. Frost bent toward him. "Pearblossom, can you hear me, can you see me, Herb?"

The roof of the cab over them, there was little danger of direct hits from the gunfire above and to a degree it was almost a moment's safe haven from it. "Hey, Captain Frost," he heard Pearblossom say, the man's voice as clear as a bell. "No, man, I can't see ya'—you're gonna have to teach me some eyepatch jokes—but do ya know any for a guy missin' both eyes? I'm blind, man."

"Oh, Jesus," Frost said, turning his face away. "Why you, man?"

"Yeah, I could ask that same question myself, Captain. But I guess it had to be somebody. My leg—it ain't there, is it?"

Frost looked down under the boiler plate. Pearblossom was right.

"Come on man, don't jive me none—I'm gettin' cold—I'm bleedin' to death and I hurt, oh mama of God do I hurt . . ."

Pearblossom could hang on for hours, Frost knew that, and there was no medical treatment in the world that would help him. Drugs might numb the pain but clearly now Frost could see that Pearblossom was burned over more than ninety percent of his body—and there was the leg.

"Do the number, Captain. My hands don't work too good or I would have already—please, Captain?"

Frost and Pearblossom both knew what was

being talked about, Frost knew that instinctively.

Frost reached under his left armpit and took out his pistol, ripping it through the trigger-guard snap. He thumbed back the hammer to full cock. "Oh, Christ, man," Frost said, his voice breaking, "I don't want to. Herb?" Frost was breathing hard as he moved the pistol's muzzle toward Pearblossom's head.

"Thank you . . ." Pearblossom whispered, his voice trailing off.

There was a loud crack from a pistol to Frost's left. He turned. Marina was in a crouch, down on her knees on the edge of the coal car, just under the protecting roof of the locomotive cab, her father's revolver in both her hands.

Frost looked away from the gun, back across the ten feet or so of flooring and down at Pearblossom. There was a bullet hole in the right side of his head well behind the temple. There was no breathing. Frost closed his friend's eyes and peeled off his own bloodstained fatigue blouse and covered the man with it.

He looked back at Marina. "I followed you when you came across the coal car, then I went back and asked my father—he's been awake since he was moved from the other car again—and he gave me the revolver. I couldn't let you suffer the way my father did over Colonel Sanchez."

She climbed down into the locomotive cab and took a tentative step toward him. Upping the safety on his pistol and shoving it in his trouser band, Frost went to her and folded her into his arms, felt her sobbing against his chest. Frost wanted to say something but his voice wasn't working. The gunfire from outside the shelter of the cab was still heavy.

Taking a last glance back at Pearblossom, Frost grabbed Marina by the hand and started toward the coal car. The gunfire was so heavy as they reached the edge of the shelter from the iron roof of the cab, Frost had to draw her back.

Controlling his voice still difficult, Frost whispered, "We'll never make it back across the coal car—they've got too many guns now. We're going to have to go under the car—it's our only chance."

Taking her hand again, the girl behind him in a low crouch, Frost glanced toward both canyon rims in turn, trying to judge which was turning out the lowest volume of fire. The noise of bullets impacting against the metal roof of the cab was intensifying. Finally Frost decided—the engineer's side of the cab, the left side.

Pulling the girl behind him, the Browning High Power 9mm in his right hand, he edged toward the left side opening. She started to speak and he held a finger to his lips, listening intently to the volume of fire trying to find a lull. Suddenly, he shoved her forward out of the cab, diving out behind her and coming down hard on his feet, just at the edge of the gorge, the forward portion of the engine still hanging over the void.

Dragging the girl behind him, Frost dove under the coal car, its first set of wheels off the track. "Come on," he rasped, crawling forward along the rails, ducking his head to avoid the axle.

He looked behind him when she winced,

"What's wrong?"

"I hit my shin against a spike that was sticking up."

"Okay," he said. "Come on!" He moved forward, stopping at the rear edge of the car. The fire volume was still heavy, apparently the terrorists on the rim of the canyon having followed them with their sights and still intent on pinning them down.

"Nifkawitz!" Frost shouted. He called the CIA man's name again as loudly as he could. After a moment, craning his neck upward toward the passenger car door on the platform above, he spotted the door opening a crack. A hail of bullets pounded against it and it slammed shut, then a few seconds later opened once more.

"Frost? That you?" It was Nifkawitz.

"No, it's Santa Claus and I can't make it down the chimney—of course it's me! We're pinned down," Frost shouted.

"What do you want me to do?" Nifkawitz shouted back through the crack in the door less than ten feet away.

"Create some kind of diversion by the back door of the car, then lay down a heavy volume of fire from here and get the door open for us. I've got Marina with me."

"Gotcha," Nifkawitz shouted back, then pulled the door closed behind him.

It was less than two minutes by the Omega on Frost's wrist, but it seemed an eternity to him. Then the door of the coach car opened and Nifkawitz and two of the Marines trained M-16s on

216

the canyon rims and started firing. Frost grabbed Marina's wrist and dragged her from under the coal car, pushing her ahead of him onto the platform, Nifkawitz in turn almost throwing her through the door to the inside. Frost, the leg wound making movement awkward, pulled himself onto the platform, slipping as his left leg started to buckle under him. The volume of terrorist gunfire was increasing again—he felt a slug tearing at his left shoulder. Looking up toward the door as he started pulling himself onto the platform again, he saw Nifkawitz, the CIA man's hands reaching out and grabbing Frost by the shoulders, wrenching him up toward the platform.

Frost didn't even get to his feet, but on his knees there at the edge of the platform threw himself forward, dragging himself through the doorway in a hail of bullets, then rolling onto his back in time to see Nifkawitz and the two Marines slam the door.

Marina helping him, Frost hauled himself to his feet, staying in a low crouch, the terrorist gunfire ripping into the passenger car from both sides. Frost glanced around him—there were perhaps some thirty-five people crowded into the rail car, most with guns in their hands firing out the windows from both sides of the aisle. Frost started down the aisle, but he felt someone grabbing at his arm. He looked around—it was the Embassy doctor, the man who'd been attending Aguillara-Garcia.

"Let me take a look at that leg," the white-haired man said firmly.

Frost looked back to the windows, shrugged and dropped back down to the floor in the center of the car. As the doctor probed the wound, Frost gritted his teeth against the pain. "Bleeding a lot," the medic said, "but clean enough. I've got some sulfa powder handy—have to do. Bullet went right through it looks like." While the doctor bandaged the leg, Marina attended the wound across his back, this too doused with antiseptic and a bandage put across it. "What about that shoulder?" the doctor said testily as Frost started to haul himself to his feet again, the leg wound bandaged.

"What about it?" Frost answered. "The bullet just grazed me—got the same thing on my wrist," and Frost showed him. "Take care of somebody who needs it—thanks."

The doctor just shook his head and moved off down the center of the car in a low crouch, not getting farther than eight feet before he stopped again to inspect one of the Embassy people, bleeding badly with a fresh headwound.

Frost looked around the car, spotted what looked like his CAR-16 leaning into a corner, snatched it then checked the serial number. It was his. He started toward the far end of the car, where Aguillara-Garcia, still on his back after the heart seizure, was resting behind an impromptu barricade made of suitcases.

Marina behind him, Frost stopped and looked at the President. His eyes were open and he seemed alert. "Thank you for sending your daughter, sir. I know better how you felt with Colonel

218

Sanchez before."

"Do you think, amigo, that we will get out of this alive?" Aguillara-Garcia said, his voice weaker than Frost remembered it.

Frost turned and looked around him a moment. Then looking back at the President, said, "I suppose it is possible. You know I derailed Commacho—it was either that or have both trains go over the gorge—he was coming too fast."

"I have learned, Captain Frost, that you do few things for poor reasons. Commacho, like you, I realize, is my friend. I was praying that he had somehow survived."

"I'll second that, but as to your question, if there is a way for us to get out alive, I can't see it."

"I will ask a favor then," Aguillara-Garcia said, "and it is something I would not ask anyone else. If the end comes, I can take my own life. I will burn in Hell for doing this, but there is no choice. I will kill Anna, as well. But I could not take the life of my—"

He started coughing on the last word and Frost said to him, "I'll do it. I don't know how, El Presidente, but I will do this thing for you. Rest easy," he added and touched the older man's hand. Aguillara-Garcia moved his hand to clasp Frost's, then whispered, "Sometimes, amigo, however strange the course of friendship runs, it always returns to the true path."

Frost nodded, then moved along toward the windows on the right side of the car as it faced the engine and coal car. He found himself beside Nifkawitz. The terrorist gunfire was coming less

219

rapidly now, but nonetheless incessant.

Frost glanced behind him. Marina was giving her father's gun back to him.

Then looking at Nifkawitz, Frost said, "Thanks for my life again, pal. Makes me feel worse and worse about that knee I gave you back in the Ambassadore's office."

"I was playing a part for Pilchner and so were you, Frost—don't sweat it. You figure we got a chance in hell of getting out of here?"

Frost looked back at Nifkawitz and shook his head. "No."

"How you want to play it?" Nifkawitz asked, his voice even and low.

"The volume of fire from the rim is a lot lower. We're stuck here and they know it. It still seems awfully important for them to get Aguillara-Garcia alive. Well, the only way I see it is when they come, hold them off as long as possible so the President can do what he plans—they used to call it the 'dutch act.'"

Nifkawitz glanced over his shoulder toward Aguillara-Garcia. "Just take out as many of the terrorists as we can on the way down, huh?"

"Yeah," Frost said, a smile crossing his lips. "Alamo time."

The minutes dragged by into more than an hour and, as best as Frost could judge it, a terrorist assault from the ground was imminent. There had been more than enough time for a large portion of their forces to move down from the canyon rims and prepare. Any hopes Frost had had of Commacho surviving and troops coming up to help them had apparently been groundless. No survivors of the train wreck? Frost hoped that wasn't the case. The ammunition supply was dwindling down rapidly and for that reason, for the last twenty minutes Frost had made everyone hold their fire. Frost had three twenty-round magazines for his CAR-16, including the one in the gun, plus two spare magazines for the Browning High Power and more or less a dozen rounds in the magazine that was already in place. One of the Marines had bought it with a stray bullet about ten minutes after Frost had joined Nifkawitz by the windows, so Frost had helped himself to the Marine's bayonet to replace his broken knife.

Earlier, too, Frost had passed around the axes and shovels from the foraging kits. The first wave of the terrorist assault would eat up most of their ammo. Once the terrorists reached the train, it would be hand-to-hand.

It was nearly three o'clock as Frost took a sip of water from the container Marina was taking around to the defenders. She touched his hand before she moved on, saying, "I am glad for the moments we had together this morning, Hank." He leaned toward her and kissed her cheek.

"Here they come!" It was one of the Marines who had shouted. Frost turned toward the window beside him, the CAR-16 in his hands, the stock telescoped out to his shoulder. From behind the train on both sides of the track and from Frost's side of the track toward the front from along the gorge, he saw them. They were moving forward slowly, rank upon uneven rank, dozens of armed men—some women too, Frost thought. There were at least a hundred, likely more he counted, plus the support fire from the canyon rim. But this had stopped for the moment.

Frost's defenders were holding their fire as Frost had told them, waiting for his signal. From outside, in heavily accented English, Frost heard a familiar voice.

"Surrender, yankee—or die."

Frost spotted the origin of the voice. It was the young student whose life Frost had spared after the terrorist street bombing. Frost shook his head and muttered to himself, "That's what I get for being a good guy." Then Frost did two things simultaneously. As he twitched the trigger of his assault rifle and shot the student neatly between the eyes across the hundred or so yards that separated them, he shouted to the defenders aboard the rail car with him, "Open fire!"

Chapter Nineteen

The initial roar of gunfire was deafening from inside the passenger coach. As the young terrorist fell under Frost's gunfire, the terrorist forces charged forward in waves. In less than a minute, Frost was already through half a magazine in the CAR-16. Hot brass from guns on either side of the car pelting him in the face, on his bare shoulder and chest, Frost concentrated his fire—semi-auto to avoid wasting ammunition—on the front ranks coming up from the sabotaged bridge by the gorge. He changed magazines and continued firing. With semi-automatic fire only, Frost and the other defenders were making most of their shots count, taking a heavy toll of the terrorist attackers.

By the time the closest of the terrorist waves was fifty yards from the train, the gunfire was starting to turn them back. In a moment more it was a full withdrawal.

A cheer went up in the railroad car as Frost shouted, "Hold your fire!" As the cheering subsided, he added soberly, "Don't waste ammo, they'll be back."

Frost looked around the car for Marina. He spotted her, helping the doctor, the flesh wound on her left shoulder from earlier up on the roof still unbandaged.

"Marina," he shouted. She turned, smiled and moved toward him along the center of the car. Once she was beside him, he put his arm around her and said, "You're going to have to stay here with me now. I made a promise to your father—"

"I guessed that," she said, her voice lifeless. "I don't want you to."

"You don't want to be captured, believe me."

"Then I will do it myself," she said, stubbornly.

Frost looked back out the window. Already he could see the terrorists starting to regroup a few hundred yards back down the track—apparently for one full-tilt frontal assault. It would cost them dearly, Frost knew, but there was no doubt they would be able to overrun the railroad car and be triumphant. He turned back to Marina. "When the time comes—Just stay beside me here—Okay?"

Resolutely nodding her head, she forced a smile,

her hands reaching out and touching his. Marina behind him then, Frost moved toward the rear door of the train, near Aguillara-Garcia. Anna was there as well, kneeling beside her husband. Frost glanced toward her but she did not appear to see him.

Throwing open the door and standing just inside it, Frost shouldered his rifle, and peering through the door toward the terrorist position, shouted to the defenders. "All right, keep to semi-automatic fire only, save handguns for twenty yards and less. When they hit the car here, keep firing toward every possible entry way, be sure of your targets. When you have no more ammo, grab a gun from someone who has been hit. When you're completely out of ammo, the muzzle of your rifle used like a spear or bayonet will do a lot of damage. Those of you with the axes and shovels, just pretend you're playing baseball and you're trying to knock heads out of the park. And," Frost added, his voice dropping, "anyone who wants to, save one last slug for yourself. These guys mutilate and torture prisoners—especially any of you women."

Frost took his eye from his sights and glanced behind him. All the people in the car—men and the few women—were motionless, listening, but their faces reading that they didn't want to hear. "And," the voice belonged to President Aguillara-Garcia, "may God bless us all and forgive us the lives we take."

Frost didn't look around. There was no more time. The last assault had started.

The first ranks of the terrorists, AK-47s blazing, were less than fifty yards away when Frost finally gave the order, "Open fire," the nearest targets falling under the withering volume of the initial volley. Frost started going after the heavy machine-gun crews, trying to prevent them setting up a hundred yards from the train in the shelter of a rock slide. Still firing semi-auto, he nailed the farthest of the machinegunners with a head shot, rolling the man back against the gun itself. As he did, he swapped magazines for the last time.

A dozen or more of the terrorists had broken through the wall of gunfire and were less than ten yards now from the train. Frost had no choice but to go for them as did Nifkawitz beside him. Both men fired—almost point-blank now—dropping half the terrorists before they reached the edge of the car platform a few feet from the doorway. Frost started to fire a burst but the CAR-16 was empty. Dropping it from his hands he ripped the Browning High Power from his trouser band and shot one terrorist in the face as he reached the doorway.

Stepping over the body, Frost was on the car platform now, firing point blank into wave after wave of terrorists. The Browning empty, Frost lashed out with the muzzle of the pistol jamming it with full force into one of the terrorist's throats as he clambered up over the railing. Taking two steps back into the car, Frost swapped magazines in the Browning and kept on firing. Nifkawitz, beside him, screamed out in pain and Frost snapped a glance to his side—the CIA man was clasping his chest with both hands, fallen back at a bizarre angle against the wall.

Frost had emptied the second to last of the Browning pistol's thirteen-round magazines, reached down and snatched up Nifkawitz's Government Model .45, fired it dry into the closing wall of terrorists, then rammed his last fresh magazine into the Browning.

Aguillara-Garcia had gotten to his feet. Frost could see him there, beside Marina, Anna standing behind him, the little Python .357 in his right hand at hip level. Frost stepped back beside them. There were perhaps fifteen people left alive or at least moving aboard the traincar now. Outside the door, Frost could see the unbroken wall of terrorist attackers, the assault stopped, the men in the lead walking slowly up the steps to the car platform.

Frost pushed Marina behind him, Aguillara-Garcia at his side. As the lead terrorist burst through, Frost and Aguillara-Garcia fired simultaneously. Man after man, the Communist terrorists fell under the pistol fire.

Frost cursed—"Dammit." The Browning was empty, as was Aguillara-Garcia's Python. Frost could hear the hammer clicking on the spent chamber. There was a dead Marine on the floor near him, an axe beside the body. Frost grabbed it up. Silently, he prayed that Marina would die during the assault. The terrorists were not six feet from Frost now, perhaps a half dozen crammed inside the doorway of the car. Holding the axe in both hands, Frost glared at them. And then they came. Frost started swinging. As the blade of his axe crashed down into the skull of the closest terrorist, Frost heard an explosion, then another. Rocket fire! Above the shouts of the terrorists, Frost could hear another sound now, the whirring of helicopter rotors in the air.

The wall of terrorists before him started falling back, Frost still swinging the axe and following after them toward the doorway. Marina beside him, he glanced skyward. The eagle symbol of Mexico was unmistakable. A squadron of Mexican Air Cavalry was overhead, already the first few of the helicopters on the ground. Outside on the battlefield, the terrorist force was in full retreat.

Frost dropped the axe and ran back into the car, searched through the bodies there until he found a loaded gun—one of the .38 Special revolvers used by the Marine Corps Embassy Guards—and ran back outside. He handed the gun to Aguillara-Garcia. "Here, use it if you have to," then, his left leg still paining him, Frost jumped to the ground behind the railcar and ran out into the battlefield. He snatched up the nearest AK-47, pulled the trigger firing into the ground to see if it was loaded and working, then caught up two spare magazines from the dead terrorist to whom it had belonged and started back down the tracks—toward the Commacho train.

As Frost ran, he could feel the bandage slipping from his leg, the pain in the wound intensifying. Somehow, it didn't matter to him. He had to know. He rounded a gentle curve and stopped. The wreck of the military train was more than he had expected. It had been a three-car military set-up, traveling fast, and apparently its own speed had just served to heighten the impact from the collision with the passenger cars from Frost's train. There were some small fires still burning in what was left of the troop cars. To plow through the wreckage to attempt to verify Commacho's death, Frost knew, would have been pointless. There were parts of bodies spread all over the ground, arms and legs burned beyond any sort of recognition.

Frost sank down to his heels there on the track, the liberated AK-47 in his right hand, riflebutt against the ground. He started asking, "Why?" But then he realized there was no one to answer the question.

Chapter Twenty

Frost always prided himself on being willing to try almost anything. And he had tried Margaritas once and now could say with utmost certainty that he didn't like them. He was the only one of the group that ordered a drink that did not contain tequilla. He told the waiter, "Rum and Coke," then leaned back and lit a cigarette. Across the table from him sat Nifkawitz, his left arm in a sling, a healthy-sized bandage on the left side of his neck. Nifkawitz was talking with the Mexican Intelligence official, Major Strauttmann; Frost had spoken with the man earlier. German father and Mexican mother, he had studied in Berlin during the late fifties, the most distinctive feature he had his bright blue eyes in the otherwise dark Mexican countenance.

To the other side of Nifkawitz, between Frost and the CIA man, sat Marina.

Though she moved her left arm stiffly, there was no other visible sign of the gunshot wound she'd suffered. Her hair up, earrings, a touch of makeup and a silk-looking low-neck black dress, Frost thought Marina looked in fact quite beautiful— perhaps as though she'd just flown in from Cannes or Paris, rather than suffered through a nearly fatal terrorist battle and a train ride on a vintage locomotive through five hundred miles of jungle. An innocent sparkle in her eyes belied the additional fact that she'd killed two men Frost had counted, albeit one a mercy killing.

"Here we sit," Frost thought, "in sunny Mexico." He smiled to himself, for it was raining outside and Mexico City, he had decided during the taxi ride with Marina to the restaurant, was not a city geared for anything but reasonably perfect weather.

The drinks came and almost before the waiter had left, Major Strauttmann raised his glass, saying, "I propose a toast—to the health of Presidente Phillipe Aguillara-Garcia," then bowing to Marina, he added, "and to the beauty of his daughter."

Frost tossed away half the contents of his glass and looked at Marina, then said, "I'll drink to that

231

any day."

"Capitan Frost," Strauttmann said. "I am still uncertain. Had you any idea that your Senor Pilchner was responsible for the terrorist activities?"

Lighting a cigarette, Frost looked across the table, saying, "No—and I don't think he was. As Nifkawitz's people found out later, Pilchner was apparently representing a small group of men in Washington who wanted peace at any price—and handing the Communists Monte Azul and Mexico by way of helping the terrorists was just a logical extension of the philosophy."

Nifkawitz interjected, "Yeah—and after Frost here accidentally got involved with the assassination of Marina's uncle, the President's brother, in Switzerland, Pilchner manipulated legitimate State Department authorities into that deal in the Swiss jail—to get Frost down to Monte Azul. Pilchner figured he could predict that Frost would do his job regardless of what he was told to the contrary, so he wasn't surprised at all when Hank kidnapped President Aguillara-Garcia and brought him along to get him out of the country. In fact, Frost was doing just what Pilchner had probably anticipated. He was using Hank—using all of us, really—to get Aguillara-Garcia out of the Presidential Palace and where his terrorist pals could lay their hands on him."

"But why was it such a personal thing between Pilchner and Hank—the whole torture thing," Marina queried, sipping at her Margarita.

Nifkawitz said, "I guess like Hank remembers

Pilchner saying before they got started—"

Frost cut him off, finishing his sentence, "—because he enjoyed it." Frost downed the rest of his drink.

"Your father," Strauttmann said, "is still planning to start a government in exile then, Senorita Aguillara-Garcia? And with your help?"

"Si. We have no way of knowing if perhaps someday it will be possible to return to our homeland, but at least we must try—we must do as Hank told my father, perhaps. We must try if nothing else to be a voice against Latin American Communism."

"You will be in danger then, Senorita," Strauttmann said.

"I will have Hank to protect me—and my father, at least for another few days until security arrangements have been made. And then, too, there are the men your government so kindly provides us."

Strauttmann waved his hand in a gesture of magnanimity.

Frost said to him, "Are there going to be any international repercussions about the rescue mission and your Army people knocking it out with those terrorists?"

"After the massive explosion of the troop train was detected by our border police, we had to investigate. And the battle site was only a few miles inside the border with Monte Azul. The Senorita's father was still technically the President of that country and so, in effect, we were entering upon his soil with his permission—let the Communist batardos—forgive me, Senorita—complain. We do not care. The units had been on alert waiting for your train to cross our border ever since Senor Nifkawitz alerted us before you even left the capitol of Monte Azul."

The waiter returned then, and Frost said, "I don't know about you guys, but after yesterday I was too tired to eat breakfast and I slept right through lunch, so I'm hungry." Marina touched his hand, smiling and after a moment he ordered for both of them.

There was more small talk about politics throughout dinner and afterward. Frost and Marina made the excuse of retiring early and left Nifkawitz and his Mexican opposite number there in the restaurant to drink the night away if they wished. Frost had already declined an invitation from Presidente Aguillara-Garcia to return to Monte Azul and lead a guerilla band against the Communists—Frost had told the President there were just too many memories there, the death of Commacho, everything.

It was a Monday night and by that following Friday Frost had plans to be back in the United States looking for a nice quiet security job and some rest. He had sixty-five thousand dollars in the bank—more money than he had ever had at one time before in his life. At the back of his mind, though, he felt slightly guilty for it with Marina beside him. He thought perhaps he might fly to London and see Bess.

He helped Marina on with the raincoat she'd worn and pulled on his own coat, then held the door for her as they went out under the canopy onto the sidewalk to hail a taxi. The rain was still pouring down heavily and it took several minutes before they found an empty taxicab.

Frost let Marina, her Spanish vastly superior, tell the driver their destination. They sat back together in the seat then and watched the late evening traffic making suicide runs through the rainy intersections. It took twenty minutes to get out of the city proper and another ten minutes to reach the country house Aguillara-Garcia had been hastily given for his personal use until other arrangements could be made.

The security around the grounds was tight and one of the guards from the small detachment of Mexican troops flashed his light in Frost's eye and then at Marina before the taxi was allowed up the drive to the front of the house. Frost paid the driver and then he and Marina ran out into the rain, up the front steps and as they reached the door it opened. The butler—a security man as well—took their sodden raincoats and Frost followed Marina into the first floor library.

They sat together for a while watching the fire burning on the hearth, then finished their drinks and went up to bed.

Marina and Frost had adjoining rooms near the head of the staircase on the second floor. Aguillara-Garcia's room—a nurse in attendance and a security man sitting outside the door—was by the end of the hallway. Anna was staying in a hotel in Mexico City itself.

Frost and Marina entered her room and

235

undressed, Frost tossing his Metalifed Browning High Power 9mm on the bed, still in the shoulder rig, the clothes over a chair. He followed Marina into the bathroom and, the water already running by the time he got there, they stepped into the shower, just standing there in the steaming hot spray and trying to get warm. After a few moments, she came into his arms, his left hand on her breasts. Her lips were warm as he felt them against his ear whispering, "Have you ever done—in the shower—you know."

"Yes," he said, perhaps less than gallant.

"Do it with me," she said, and then he felt her hands on him. Leaning there against the steamed-over tiles under the spray of the shower head, Frost had to support her so she could stand up on her toes—it was the only way she was tall enough for him to enter her. Her thighs, her breasts rubbed against him. She started to lose her balance once and he slipped out of her, then they came together once more and as he felt her nails digging into his back, together they reached the moment they'd wanted, then just stood there for a while, the water pouring down on them, their breathing in short gasps. He kissed her.

After a while, they got out of the shower, went through the sliding glass doors and she dried his back. Naked, he walked across the room, found his cigarettes in the pocket of his jacket and listened to her singing softly as she tried doing something with her wet hair in the bathroom behind him.

He lit a Camel and dropped the Zippo lighter on the bedside table beside the fresh pack of cigarettes he'd started, then walked toward the window, stopping for a moment to look at her as she came to join him. She was wearing a beltless, floor-length yellow robe, of the same material as the pale yellow towel she had wrapped over her hair.

"Don't you have a robe?" she asked. "You'll catch pneumonia."

"Sorry, I'll buy one tomorrow," he said, the smile-frown lines in his face creasing into a smile. He put his hand on her waist and kissed her lightly on the lips, then walked over to the window, pulling the drape aside and looking down into the rain-drenched courtyard.

"Come over by the bed," Frost heard Marina whispering behind him.

As he started to let the drape slip back into place he caught it, took a step closer to the window and peered intently directly below them.

"Hell," Frost rasped.

He made it across the room in two strides, his hands shuffling the covers on the bed. "My gun—where did you put my gun?"

"What's the matter, Hank?" she said, her voice sounding frightened.

He grabbed her shoulders. "Never mind that. My gun? Where?"

"Under your coat, on the chair." Frost let go of her and ran to it, fumbled open the thumbreak on the shoulder holster, then holding the rear of the harness ripped the Browning from the leather through the trigger guard snap.

"What is it, Hank?" she half screamed.

Frost glanced around the room, stepping into

his pants as he said, "Go lock yourself in the bathroom—and don't stand by the door. I just spotted a half dozen men in military gear running across the courtyard."

By the time Frost reached the doorway, there was already automatic weapons fire from the hallway. He stepped through the doorway.

The Browning High Power in his right fist fired twice, the slugs hammering into the chest of a black-clad commando-type with a submachine gun in his hands running from the head of the stairs.

Two more men were behind him. They had to be Castro's men, Frost thought—after Aguillara-Garcia. Frost fired, the first two rounds catching the nearest assassin in the crotch and dropping him to the carpeted hall floor like a rock. As Frost swung the muzzle of his Browning toward the second man, the submachine gun opened up and Frost felt himself thrown back against the bedroom door, the pistol flying from his hand. As he sank to the floor, the assassin ran past him.

From the first floor, Frost could hear the sounds of more automatic weapons fire.

Frost turned his head. The guard by Aguillara-Garcia's doorway lay on the floor, apparently dead—the first SMG blast he'd heard in the hallway.

Frost dragged himself across the floor—three feet more and the Browning would be back in his hand. He had to use only his right hand, his left hand on his stomach, holding in his guts Frost thought.

238

Frost kept moving. From inside Aguillara-Garcia's room he heard a heavy pistol shot, then a long burst from the submachine gun. Frost finally reached his pistol, got it into his right hand, and as the assassin ran from Aguillara-Garcia's room, Frost pulled the trigger. Emptying the pistol up into the killer's head.

Frost dragged himself to his knees, but couldn't stand up, the pistol hanging limply in his right hand by the trigger guard. The gunfire from the first floor had stopped, and after a moment two of the Mexican soldiers ran down the hallway past him and into Aguillara-Garcia's room.

The doorway from the bedroom opened on Frost's left.

"Marina," Frost shouted. "Help me up—hurry."

She bent down to him, the towel falling from her hair to the blood-stained carpet.

Frost dropped his pistol on the floor, supporting himself against the wall with his right hand, his blood-stained left hand on Marina's shoulder. Frost glanced down at his stomach. He hurt badly, but he'd been wounded before. The bleeding was starting to slow.

He stopped in the doorway of the room Aguillara-Garcia had used. Leaning up against the doorframe, he whispered to Marina, "I'm all right, kid. Go to him."

She looked at Frost a moment, then ran across the room to her father, the President's chest and abdomen a mass of wounds. The nurse was standing there beside the dead president, her eyes

239

wide with terror. Frost saw her look in his direction, then the nurse started toward him. Frost sank to his knees by the doorframe and leaned his head against it, the nurse already beside him trying to see to his wounds. Frost closed his eye and whispered something, his voice barely audible. The nurse beside him said, "What did you say, Capitan?"

Frost repeated himself—"What the hell was the use of all this?" Nobody answered him.